WHEN YOU WERE]

ANNA-KAT TAYLOR

WHEN YOU WERE

mine

Anna-Kat Taylor

ANNA-KAT TAYLOR

COPYRIGHTS

Copyright reserved @ 2023 by Anna-Kat Taylor

All rights reserved.

No part of this book may be reproduced in any form or shape without written permission from the author except for the brief quotations in a book review.

The characters and events portrayed in this book are pure fiction. Any resemblance to places, events, or real people, living or dead, is entirely coincidental and not intended by the author.

ANNA-KAT TAYLOR

TRIGGER WARNING

This book may contain triggering scenes that include forced marriage, domestic abuse, and sexual assault.

If you think you may be triggered by any of this content, please do not read this book, if you do so, it will be on your own responsibility.

ANNA-KAT TAYLOR

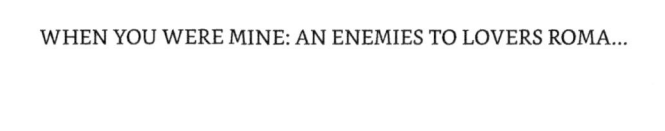

*To all the women out there who believe in second
chances after an abusive relationship.
You did it, now don't let the past haunt you.*

ANNA-KAT TAYLOR

PROLOGUE

They say ghosts often don't remember that they've died.

I can't help but wonder, could I be one?

Could I be so broken that I can't tell between fantasy and reality anymore? Could I be stuck in limbo, stuck in this cruel place forever without an escape?

Death it's supposed to be freeing, but what if for me it was just a curse?

I stare at my husband's coffin who's about to be put 6 feet underground and I can't shed a tear. I hadn't shed a single one since they came to my door and told me that my husband's car breaks gave up and he had an accident, which led to him passing later at the hospital.

When I opened the door while the red and blue lights illuminated his entire hollow house, I knew deep down that the worst happened, but I refused to believe it until the police officer actually spoke the words.

I quickly fell onto my knees and let out the out heart wrenching scream, and they must've thought that the pain was too hard to bear because of the news I got, when in reality there was a different fear stretching in my chest.

Sebastian and I got married when I was just 24 years old and that's only 3 years ago, although it feels like a lifetime has passed since that horrible May evening.

It feels like I've been with this man my entire life but when Sebastian Dawson landed his eyes on me, he decided that he had to have me forever, so we got married a few months after we met.

He's got a lot of people attending his funeral and most of them seem to disapprove of me being here to say goodbye to my husband like I'm some kind of mistress, and that's just fucking horrible, but they've always been horrible.

They've all hated me since the moment they met me because they could never understand why a 24-year-old young woman would get married to a 39-year-old man, if not for his money.

It's always for the money, isn't it?

Yes, Sebastian Dawson was loaded, with a marketing company worth millions and investments all over the country. He didn't build it from the ground up though, his father handed it to him and his brother before he passed and Sebastian took it to different heights, but now it is his younger brother Asher's turn to take care of it.

The brother who's now standing a mere few feet across from me and throws daggers at me while I wonder if my body would still react to his touch the way it used to.

When Asher thought that I had chosen his

brother over him, he left Sebastian in charge here in the US, skipped town, and moved to London. I was equally devasted and relieved because I don't know if I would've been able to survive this if he were still in my life.

It's a lot easier to fake and pretend when the other person hates you from a few thousand miles away, just as I guess is a lot easier to believe a story from so far.

But here he is now, staring at me with hatred in his grey steel eyes. Eyes that used to look at me with love and lust in them, now stare at me like I shouldn't exist in this world anymore for what I did to him.

And worst thing is, I deserve it. I hate myself too.

"You shouldn't be here, Hayley," is the first thing he says to me, a year later with a ticking jaw and blue ocean eyes shining with anger and hatred.

That fucking jawline.

Those damn dimples.

He's right, I shouldn't be here, and I should avoid him at all costs, yet here I am, rooted on the spot, taking him in. Remembering every curve of his muscled body. Remembering how my favorite thing was the way A dress shirt hugs his back, but how I would take it off him and wear it instead, so I could gawk at that broad back.

I push down the tears that threaten to spill over and laugh in his face to keep my calm. I can't show any type of emotion right now, while everyone is watching me with hawk eyes, but it physically hurts to look at him.

Play it brave, Hayley. Don't show him the power he has over you. "You mean at my husband's funeral? Who are you anyway to tell me where I should and shouldn't be?!"

He chuckles angrily and my heart skips a beat. *Damn you traitor.* "You are in no position to question me, sweetheart. I want you out of this city as soon as the casket is down below. You don't belong here. You never did and you've done enough harm to my family, by killing my brother. So, it's better you go, before I lose my temper and do something I'll regret later," he retorts angrily, and I want to laugh or move or do anything else but stare.

I can only stare and lose myself in his eyes. His words cut deep and manage to open every single scar and wound but I'm not losing this fight.

"I'm starting to wonder what I saw in you. You're such a rude brute," I reply and lift the corners of my mouth with a smile, ignoring every word he throws at me and keeping my head held high.

He will not see me cry.

I don't have it in me to be hurt by him anymore. I don't think I have any more fight left in me. I could as well be buried next to Sebastian, because he killed me a long time ago anyway.

Asher only continues to stare at me with a hardened gaze. "Is that why you chose my brother?"

Now I'm the one who clenches her jaw and looks

away because I can't tell him the truth. Not yet anyway.

I shouldn't have said that. Shouldn't have brought up our past, but I couldn't help it.

I knew that seeing him will only bring up heartbreak, but I had to come. I had to be here and spit on his brother's grave. "I had nothing to do with your brother's death, Ace," I add in a cold tone, deflecting his question again.

Ace.

My Ace.

God, he's going to hate me calling him that again, so a tiny smile lights my face.

"Is that why you stand here looking like a stone-cold bitch? Brakes don't just stop working, Hayley!" he argues and I just stare. I look at him, even tilt my head a bit and hold my black suede hat so it doesn't fall off.

He's right in everything he says.

I am stone cold.

I'm fucking numb and can't feel a thing and that's because of his precious brother and I couldn't care less about his brakes, but I sure as hell am glad that they failed.

I sure as hell am glad that I didn't have to do it myself and become a murderer.

Because Sebastian Dawson was a piece of shit.

And I am glad he's gone.

Because that means I'm finally free or so I hope.

ONE | HAYLEY

PRESENT DAY

It's been a year since my husband's been put to rest, and here I am, back in Westport, having to deal with ghosts from my past. The will is ready for reading so our lawyer has called me back to the city.

The city I hoped I never had to step into again.

A year ago, I had the nerve to think I was free and that I could go back to being the girl I was before I married Sebastian.

I was so wrong.

That girl doesn't exist anymore and the new girl stares at me with hollow eyes every time I look in the mirror.

She's utterly broken and unable to be fixed.

"Miss Dawson, thank you for coming to meet me on such short notice," she speaks, but that's just professional bullshit because she called me a month ago with the request and I've been thinking about it ever since. However, I nod politely and sit down in front of her.

I'm not in the mood to argue with her, but I do correct her. "It's Marshall now, not Dawson." I remind her, just as I did when she called. I never liked her before, and this is why. She's just another nosy bitch who always advised Sebastian to make me sign a prenup, which I did, but wasn't entirely the way he intended it to be.

She smiles curtly. "Apologies then, wasn't sure if you kept the name or not. Most people keep their husband's names especially when the husband was so wealthy." She explains and I can't help but notice the bitterness in her tone. I will never understand how these stupid women used to throw themselves at such a piece of shit as my late husband.

Just as I'll never understand why I was the lucky gal he simply had to marry.

"I'm not like most people," I shrug it off with the lift of one shoulder.

I can see that surprised her a lot more than the fact that I haven't kept that stupid name.

I want nothing to do with the Dawsons anymore and that name should've been buried with my husband, but unfortunately, there's one Dawson left.

One Dawson who swore to have me buried right next to the other one.

"Right. Miss Marshall, I'll make this brief and won't keep you for long. As per his will, you now own his mansion, his house in Aspen, a 50 percent stake in his company and a 15 million dollars account. A little bit of everything he had."

I love how she says his for everything. She's not wrong though. They were his and I want nothing to do with them. I'm not here for the fortune.

I want nothing to do with his name, his house, or his company. I'll burn it all one by one.

He willingly left me everything so I can now understand how much he hated Asher and his mother for ruining his parent's marriage, so he didn't want Ace to get everything.

"Thanks, Miss Jennings."

It's not a secret to me that Sebastian was a troubled psychopath, but it is to the world. There has to be an underlying reason why he would leave me everything.

I exit the restaurant with the papers in my hand and I'm sure there will be pictures on Instagram before I make it to the sidewalk, but that's okay. This time, I stand tall and walk in a straight line, one leg in front of the other with my head held high.

Although he shouldn't be the first person that comes to mind now that I'm in town, he is and there's nothing I can do about it. I think it's been long enough, and he needs to know the truth before I disappear again, so I flag down a taxi.

He needs to know that I never chose his brother, he chose me and when that happened, I had no say in what happened next.

"DBSA tower, please," I say to the driver as soon as I climb in his back seat. He knows where that is because everyone does.

Dawson's marketing company is number one in the country and a landmark in this town.

I'm not sure if Sebastian didn't know that I met his brother before him, or he just was that big of a psychopath and didn't care. He was a selfish, psychopathic prick and just before our rushed wedding, Asher disappeared abroad and never came back until his brother's death.

Could that be why Sebastian left me half the company? Just so that his brother didn't get full control? Or maybe he was that obsessed with me?

I arrive at the tower faster than I thought it'll take, and I exit the cab. I look up at the size of this thing and I get claustrophobic just thinking that I have to go all the way up to the offices, where I know my nemesis enjoyed that comfy chair for a year, thinking that he got rid of me without a fight and that everything belongs to him.

It doesn't.

"Oh, I'm here to fight, Ace. I won't let you blame me anymore."

I'm here to burn it to the ground and I won't let anything stop me, not even an old fire that sparks to life just by thinking at him.

I blow out a deep breath and start heading toward the reception where I find a young lady working at the desk. "Hi, welcome to DBSA, do you have an appointment?"

"No, but that's because I don't need one. I own half of this building. My name's Hayley Marshall, previously Dawson."

"I'm sorry, Miss Marshall but I can't let anyone in without an appointment."

Good thing this doesn't have to go on because before I can reply, Asher is the next person walking through the revolving doors, and even though he steals my breath away and makes my heart beat faster, I swallow the lump in my throat and keep my calm.

It takes a minute before he looks our way and recognizes me, the realization making him halt in his steps. "What are you doing here?" he grits out between clenched teeth and reaches me in a few powerful strides. "Let's go upstairs, I don't want anyone else to see you." He grabs my arm and leads me toward the elevator.

When inside, I break free with a bristle and put some distance between us, unable to bear being so close to him and his intoxicating perfume.

I hoped seeing him wouldn't still be so hard to endure. That my heart wouldn't react the way it did, but of course I was wrong.

Just as wrong as I was when I decided to come here and face him alone.

I don't know if it's possible, but he looks even better than he did before. While I'm quickly approaching my thirties, Asher is almost 33 years old and it seems that aging only makes him look better, stronger, and more mature. His built seems bigger now and although he's wearing a wool jacket, I can still see his muscles bulge through it. He's always been a lean man. His normally clean and sharp jawline is now got a subtle stubble that makes him look meaner when he frowns.

"It's good to see you too, Ace," I whisper under my breath and wait for his reaction. He hates it when I call him that because it reminds him of the worst night of his life.

When he lost me.

The night he had to leave me alone at their company party, and his brother, Sebastian spotted me, and our fates changed forever.

"Don't you dare call me that!" he snarls and loosens his tie a little bit. Watching those tattooed fingers do the motion makes me grit my teeth and clench my thighs together.

Damn it, he has the same effect on me even after so many years. My body heats up at the sight of those tattooed sleeves and I have to swallow the lump in my throat. I don't remember his arms being so full of ink, but damn, it looks good on his muscles, and I find myself wishing I could trace a finger along his arm.

The elevator stops and I realize we haven't stopped in the office, but in his penthouse, and I swallow hard, unable to move.

No, no, no. I can't be here!

I don't want to be here.

This is the last place on earth where I should be alone with Asher Dawson, and he damn well knows it. That's exactly why he brought me here.

I really shouldn't be here, and as if he's sensing my hesitation, he teases, "What, you don't like the view? I remember you used to love it while I fucked you from behind, right against those windows," he whispers behind my ear and points at the all-glass living room making me shudder.

That's exactly why I don't want to be here and discuss business. This is the one place where I felt safe, loved, and protected but it looks like that's not the case anymore.

This is the one place I could come to in my mind, because it was my safe place.

It's the one place where I felt cherished and worshiped while he made love to me like I was the most beautiful woman in the world. All that's gone now and what's left is lies, secrets, and hate.

So much hate, that I feel it crawl against my skin.

"If you want to talk, I'll be in my office but I'm not doing it here!" I snarl at him and press floor 17, but he holds the doors open when they're about to close and pulls me inside the penthouse.

"Your office?" he growls and towers over me with a feral look on his face.

I take a step back and look him dead in the eyes, keeping as calm and professional as I can. "Yes, I'll be requesting an office in the company because as of today, I own Sebastian's half of it." I push the papers in my hand at his chest and he quickly scans through them, before he throws them on the floor.

"I always knew you were a gold-digging bitch, but this won't go well for you, Hayley. I'll make sure of it." His eyes are a blaze that could burn me alive, but it's something I have to do and if he decides to fight me, then he'll go down with their empire.

"Is that why you think I'm here, Asher? For the money? When Sebastian died, I promised I'd leave and never return to this town because being here always made me miserable. You know, I just found out an hour ago that your brother left half of everything to me, and I want none of it. I want nothing to do with you or your fucking name, but before I distance myself from it, I need to make sure he sees from whatever hell hole he's in, that he chose the wrong bitch to destroy."

I say each word with as much truth in my eyes as possible and when I see Asher's surprise in his eyes, I know I won this fight even though he continues to look at me with disgust.

I don't want him anymore.

I don't need him anymore because I stopped waiting for him to save me a long time ago.

"Your brother was a piece of shit, Asher, and when I'm done, I'll make sure everyone knows that because he doesn't deserve to die with a clean name after everything that he's done to me. He ruined my life. He ruined me and I'll be damned if he gets to remain a Saint." I say through gritted teeth and wipe away at an angry tear that escaped at the corner of my right eye.

Asher's so taken aback by my words that he doesn't even realize when I step into the elevator, and now the doors close between us, giving me enough time to breathe.

Alone in the confinement of the lift, I release the breath I didn't even know I was holding in and grab the pole to steady myself. I feel like I'm going to faint. Asher Dawson is not a man to be made angry while on the 20th floor of a building because you might find yourself flying out of those big, clean windows of his, but I couldn't be silent anymore.

When the lift stops at the 17th floor, I get out and head for the reception. I have no idea who to speak with, but I quickly recognize Milo, Seb's assistant. "Hayley? Wow, you look so different, I almost didn't recognize you," he smiles and hugs me briefly.

Of course, I look different. I couldn't stand the dark hair my ex-husband loved so much or the green contacts he forced me to wear, so I dyed my hair blonde, the color I was when he met me, and removed the contacts, going back to my hazel eyes, changing my appearance completely.

"I get that a lot lately. Listen, I need an office so I can hide away while I'm here, can you help? Make it big and with a nice view, I own half of this after all," I say with a grin, knowing that I've shocked him enough with the news, that he'll be my puppy now.

Milo's always been a snake, but I need at least one person in my corner, so I'll have to be careful so he won't bite.

He nods in understanding and leaves to find me a space in this place, leaving me alone in the lobby. It doesn't take long until Asher catches up with me and for the second time in the same day, he grabs my arm and pulls me into what seems to be the conference room.

"Please don't do this, Hayley. Don't make this harder for the both of us, I don't want you here!" He says in a calm tone, and I just stare at him. That's all I can do in this minute. I've been in this town for less than a day and I'm already exhausted.

I shake my head and blow out a deep breath. "You're right in one aspect. It is hard. It's so fucking hard to have you looking at me like that when I've done nothing to you. When I'm the one who suffered through it all while you were thousands of miles away fucking anything with two legs."

"That's the problem. You didn't do anything to me. You didn't fucking pick me," he starts shouting again and I'm starting to lose my fighting spirit. Do I really want to do this, fight him every step of the way, and every minute of the day?

I'm not a fighter. I never was, because if I had been one, I wouldn't have been so afraid of Sebastian. Maybe I would've fought back, and who knows, maybe even won.

"I swear Ace, sometimes you're so fucking stupid. You own half of this company, you had just as much money as your brother, yet you accuse me of choosing him because he had money." I say before I can stop myself.

He frowns and bites out in a venom laced tone. "Why did you choose him, then?"

I swallow. I shouldn't have said that. If I want to do this, if I want to destroy his legacy, Asher can't know the truth. He can never know any of it, regardless of how much pain it causes me.

"Why don't you figure it out, smart guy? Looks like my office might be ready," I say when I spot Milo and start walking toward the door. "Oh, Asher? I'm here to stay. I'm here to keep my promise, unlike you."

HAYLEY

FOUR YEARS AGO

When Jennifer made plans for her birthday party or better said, the few of us getting wasted, it didn't include a hard ass flu taking over me. Although I feel a lot better tonight, I'm just too exhausted to do this and feel like an old lady about to pass out. I'd rather do anything else in the world than go to a busy and overcrowded club.

I check my face in the bathroom mirror to make sure I look nice enough for a night out and smile in approval. Okay, the power of makeup is real, and no one would ever know that I'm less than 100 percent. Like my girl Rihanna said, 'Pretend'.

The black, tight, wool dress I chose to wear is hugging my body nicely and the ankle boots make me 3 inches taller. It's all I need to feel confident in the state I am and to at least not hate everyone around me for the next few hours.

This flu will get the best of me if I don't fight the tiredness and the urge to curl up on the sofa and watch Netflix for days on end.

Jennifer comes into the room with a cheerful smile on her pale face and squeals. "We're going to have so much fun. This club, Intense, is new in town and is owned by this marketing mogul and his brother. Oh, they both look so dreamy, I swear. Maybe we can each take one of them home." She chuckles and spays a ton of perfume.

"Jennifer Sinclair, please tell me you didn't choose this place for the way the owners look. They most probably won't be there, and even if they will be, they wouldn't give a flying shit about two broke college girls," I laugh at her and run my fingers through my blonde curls to smooth them out. Good thing I wore my heatless curler last night, so I didn't have to spend more time curling my hair.

It's so like Jennifer to know everything the tabloids write even if we're very busy with college work.

She values her reading time as much as I value my TV time and that's why we're the perfect roommates because I can have the TV all to myself while she reads her magazines and dark romance books. She even tried to rope me into reading the latter, but it grossed me out so much that I couldn't make it through the first sex scene.

Forced anything isn't for me. I'm a fluffy romance girl, although I don't read as much as I used to.

"Naah, I have a free table from their marketing campaign. It didn't include a meet and greet, unfortunately," she says with a scrunch of her nose. I burst out laughing and that makes my head pound with a migraine.

Fuck! Why am I so easy to control? I should've kept my ground and choose another day to celebrate her birthday.

I just want to curl up on the sofa and read a good book, maybe a dark romance, and not go out to a new fancy club, but I can't let my friend down, so I suck it up, swallow my pain and take a few deep breaths. "Okay, let's go before I trade your birthday for a hockey boyfriend."

We both grab our jackets and purses and exit the apartment we share with giggles. I swear we're acting like schoolgirls when we're both seniors in college.

When we get outside, the Uber car Jennifer ordered is already waiting for us and we both jump on the back seat.

"You think Julianna will show up?"

"I don't know, Jen. Do you want her to?" I ask her with a frown. They broke up a few weeks back, but she lost the battle with herself and called her a couple of days ago to invite her out with us to this new club.

She thinks about her answer for a long time. "I have no idea what I want, hence why I called her when I promised I wouldn't."

I chuckle and lay my head on the headrest for a minute. I close my eyes briefly, but I don't get to relax for a very long time because we arrive at the club and have to get out of the car.

Jennifer lets out a squeal as soon as she sees the fancy sign of the club. She's definitely very excited about this but I find it very hard to share her enthusiasm with this raging migraine that feels like someone hammers nails into my brain.

We enter the club after we've passed through the security guys, and I'm being greeted by Jason Derulo's Slow Low. It makes me smile and sway my hips to the rhythm for a few seconds before we find our friends sitting at a very private table at the back of the club.

A VIP table that we'd never afford if it wasn't a for Jennifer's win raffle win or whatever it was.

Score, Jennifer, I guess.

Our friends greet us with cheers and whistles, making us laugh wholeheartedly.

My friend Jason grabs my had and pulls me to sit next to him, and that's when I lock eyes with the most gorgeous, enormous, and beautiful man I've ever seen. He watches me with a grin and a stare that heats up my skin and makes my mouth go dry. A smile pulls at my lips, but I avert my gaze unable to keep up with the intensity and the warmth that spread all the way between my thighs.

"What are you ladies drinking?" Dylan asks and stands up, ready to head toward the bar.

I shake my head in response and Jen chooses a Cosmo to start the night off, making me laugh. This is a lot nicer than I was expecting it to be, but I'm suddenly very aware of *his* eyes watching my every move and I feel my cheeks turning pink under his stare, so I try my best to not look his way, but of course, I fail, and I smile when he winks at me, happy that I couldn't resist the urge to look in his direction.

No, no, no, Hayley.

Now it's not the time to fall for a dangerous-looking guy with tattooed arms and a piercing blue gaze. My future is too important to mess it up because of a guy who will most probably fuck me and then toss me away like a piece of cloth. They all do that, and he definitely doesn't look like he can be the exception.

Good guys don't look the way he does.

It's my last year and before the bar exam, I can't lose my head over a guy. It's not who I am, and I was always proud that compared to Jen, no guy caught my attention, or girl for that matter.

Before she discovered than she's more into girls than guys, Jen slept with her fair share of dudes, while scolded me for being such a Granma and not enjoying the sex life as much as she did. I guess I'm just content with my toys and my fingers because the very few boys I tried to date, disappointed me too badly for me to want to find my man.

If I'm meant to love, it'll happen without having to look for it. It'll happen when it's supposed to, and if it doesn't, I'll have my career to keep me busy.

TWO | ASHER

PRESENT DAY

This fucking woman is here to play with my soul, and I can't do anything about it.

A ghost from my past, here to haunt my present. I thought I was over her, but man was I wrong. As soon as we locked eyes and I saw that hazel gaze again, I almost wanted to smile at the sight and had to use every ounce of strength in me to not do that.

My heart became all mushy as if it recognized her erratic heartbeats when I got close to her and all I wanted to do was kiss every inch of her face and her body.

I missed her even though I never thought I'd see her back in Westport. After my brother's funeral, she disappeared without a trace and I always wondered what happened to her, so here she is a year later, ready to destroy me but I have a feeling that we're going to destroy each other.

She returned to her blonde hair color and hazel eyes, a combination that wrecked my heart all those years ago and it makes it flutter back to life now. I never understood why she kept dyeing her hair and wearing those contacts when she was so much more beautiful natural.

I never understood a lot of things when it concerned her and the things she'd said and done.

She's wearing a tight midi dress that has been making my pants extremely uncomfortable since I laid eyes on her and I'm a damn hypocrite for saying I don't want her here because she might've had something to do with my brother's death, when the real reason is that I don't trust myself around her.

Like right now, when my dick thinks for me and all I want to do is have my hands wrapped around her hair and her lips wrapped around my cock.

Fuuck!

Clenching my jaw, I stroll into my office and sit on the brown chair. I press the call button on my desk phone to reach for my assistant. "Mickayla, can you come to my office please?"

I blow out a deep breath and adjust the bulge in my pants because it became painful. Mick comes into view, and I grunt. "Close the door and come here." I gesture her to come closer and she knows exactly what she needs to do because it's not the first time.

The first time I gave in on her advances was just after I'd seen Hayley at my brother's funeral, and we'd been doing this since then. She's a good fuck whenever I need release, so I don't need to deal with dining and dating and all the other crap.

So here I am, a year later, just as affected by her presence as ever. "I need you to be a good secretary and spread your legs for me," I say, and she looks happier than she should be.

It's clear I use her, but here she is, satisfying me every time. I don't treat her nicely, and I don't care if she comes or not.

She quickly reaches for my belt and once my dick's free, she wraps a perfectly manicured hand around it to give it a few strokes before she takes me in her mouth. I moan and grab the back of her head to get better access to her mouth. She gags in response, and I close my eyes but when Hayley's face pops in my head I snap them open.

A second later I pull out of the woman's mouth and instruct her to sit on the desk. I hike her skirt up on her hips while I wrap my dick in latex and then thrust her in a slow movement, making her moan in pleasure.

I keep my thrusts in a rhythm that brings both of us pleasure and lose myself in the high of the sex until the door suddenly opens and the woman I fantasize about freezes in the doorway. I have a secluded office so no one else passes by unless they need to see me, which is not very often.

So when Hayley comes into view, I'm both shocked and thrilled, and my pleasure intensifies by 100 percent. I look her straight in the eyes with a smirk plastered on my face while I continue to pump into the woman that moans my name and reaches between us to rub her clit.

"Yes, Asher. Yes, I'm coming," my assistant screams but my entire focus is on Hayley and how her eyes just widened, and her lips parted. Did I even see her thighs clench?

She enjoys this as much as I do. Fuck, that's hot.

My entire body hums to life at the sight of her parted lips.

"You like that?" I ask with a husky voice and thrust harder and deeper, knowing I'm hitting a spot that not many men can.

"Yes, right there," Mick screams and starts shaking in my arms, consumed by her orgasm.

I, however, can only focus on Hayley's body and how it reacts to seeing me fuck another woman by how she clenches her thighs together.

With that view, I lose my mind and come with a few deep thrusts, all while I hold Hayley's gaze and throw her a brutal smile.

When I'm done, I take the condom off, throw it in the bin by the desk, and tuck myself back in.

Mick jumps off the desk and pushes her skirt down on her hips. "Excuse you? Were you here the entire time?" she shouts at Hayley like she owns the damn building, but I assume that's why she's sleeping with her boss.

"Mick, meet your new boss, Hayley Dawson," I say with a motion toward the woman still frozen in the doorway and take a seat back on my chair with a satisfied grin. Mick, on the other hand, looks terrified when she runs out of the room.

I laugh. "Did you enjoy the view?"

"I'm glad you're having fun, Asher, but I'm not here to watch porn, I can do that at home and have two fingers between my legs, without having to watch your lousy performance," she retorts and walks slowly toward me, and I have to admit that her sassy retort surprized me.

I rise from my chair and round my desk until I stand a few inches from her. "So, you haven't imagined that it was you underneath me? Because I sure as hell got off on thinking it was you." I whisper near her face, and enjoy the angry rise and fall of her chest.

She swallows and moists her lips but pretends to be cringed about my insinuation. "You're disgusting, Asher. When did you turn into this vicious man?"

"Say whatever you want, but don't you dare deny that you won't get off thinking about me tonight."

With an exasperated groan, she turns around and exits the office so fast I can barely contain my laughter. Whatever she came in here for, she probably forgot all about it as soon as she saw us.

My desk phone rings, and I pick it up with a smile. "Mr Dawson, I'm calling to remind you of your lunch meeting with Miss Diaz in 10 minutes."

"Thanks, Mick. I appreciate it," I reply with a sigh and run a hand through my chiselled hair. I check my watch and make my way toward the lobby. The restaurant I'm supposed to meet Miss Diaz in is just across the street, but I have to make sure I'm there before her.

My work ethic is that on time is late.

I make it through our floor without seeing

Hayley and I don't know how I feel about it, but when I get to the ground floor lobby, I spot her chatting with the receptionist and my blood starts rushing to my groin.

Shit.

She spots me immediately as if she can feel my presence and starts walking toward me, but I continue on my way outside because, in all fairness, I am busy.

"You're going out for lunch?" she asks with a sweet smile and falls in step next to me.

I hold the door open for her. "I am."

Maybe I shouldn't have but my mama raised me well.

"Can I join you?"

I stop in my tracks and turn to look at her. "What are you doing?"

"I'm trying to go get some lunch. You?" she says sweetly and gives me those damn doe eyes that I could never resist.

"No. What are you doing thinking we're friends? Nothing's changed, Hayley. I still want you out of my company and just because you wormed your way in, doesn't mean I have to welcome you with open arms," I grit out and proceed to walk toward the restaurant with a clenched jaw and a tense body because this is starting to feel too familiar. and I can't do familiar right now. I can't let her play with my head.

"Our company and I'm not going anywhere. Now, you're right, let's stop pretending we're friends, it's not working anyway. I know about your meeting, I'm coming with you, and there's nothing you can do about that," she retorts and straightens her back.

How the hell did she find out? Did she really pursue my assistant? "You just cost Mick her job."

She bursts out laughing and I have to stop her before she gets run over by a car. I give her the stink eye and raise a brow. "Job or blowjob?"

"You're crazy." I laugh instantly and regret it quickly afterward.

She makes it so fucking easy to be around her and I hate her for it.

I hate myself too, for being so weak.

ASHER

FOUR YEARS AGO

Her smile is like sunshine, and it brightens up the entire dark room. She licks her pink lips every few seconds and I find myself having to adjust to that movement, to hide what she's doing to me.

How am I so affected by this girl? I'm usually so laid back and immune to their charms, unless I need a good fuck, so what kind of magic is she using to keep my attention drawn onto her full and sensual hips.

Before she entered the club I own with my brother, I was bored out of my mind waiting for the guy who didn't seem to be bothered to show up and couldn't wait to find a willing girl and get out of there, but as soon as she walked in, my plans changed completely, and I find myself wanting to stay here and watch her forever.

She is just as interested in me as I am in her and it's easy to guess that from the way she turns her eyes at me every few seconds and a smile pulls at the corners of her mouth. That mouth could easily be the wet dream of any guy in this room and an image forms in my head, making me moan.

Shit!

Did I just picture her sucking my dick and it made my situation worse?

I'm acting like a horny teenager, and I almost can't believe it.

I'm here because my brother couldn't make it, but now I'm completely oblivious to whatever conversation my friends are having because this woman has my complete attention on her full lips and her curvy body since the moment she started swaying her hips on that damn song.

She walked in like she owns the place and the confidence emanating from her is probably the reason why I can't seem to be able to look away. Not that I want to, no. I need to keep my eyes on her and those two guys she's with because I don't like the way he's watching her every move, just like I do.

Suddenly she rises on her feet and with a grimace on her face, and heads for the bathroom with wobbly feet. I have been watching her for the past twenty minutes and she didn't drink anything but water, however, that could've been spiked just as well as an alcoholic beverage, so I find myself following her with worry.

The queue to the women's bathroom is longer than 10 women so she suddenly changes her mind and turns on her heel, bumping into me with a whimper and when she loses her balance, I have to catch her.

It might sound like a cliché, but I wouldn't want it to happen any other way.

"I'm so sorry, I didn't see you," she says apologetically but as soon as she lifts her eyes and recognizes me, she frowns and stands on her own two feet, away from my touch.

"Not a problem. Always happy to save a damsel in distress," I say with a grin on my face, and she takes a step back to put some distance between us. Damn, she's tiny and short, my 6'5 makes me feel like a giant compared to her 5'5.

"I wouldn't have fallen if you weren't so close behind me. Were you following or something?" she snaps and narrows her eyes at me, making me burst out in laughter. The club is dark, but it seems like she's got the most beautiful hazel eyes.

"Yes, I was. I followed to make sure that you're okay. Are you?" I ask after I manage to contain my amusement.

She grins a second later, and that leaves me puzzled.

"Are you admitting that you've been watching me?" she asks with a smile and a raised eyebrow.

"I never said I didn't, nor will I even deny it. I quite enjoyed watching you. You're worth every minute that I spent looking at you," I say exactly what I'm thinking, and her smile only gets bigger.

Damn, I need to taste those lips. As soon as that thought crosses my mind, I act on it. I grab the back of her head with my left hand and smash my lips onto hers. She gasps in surprise but doesn't fight me, and when her small palm rests on the middle of my chest, just on top of my fast-beating heart, I groan and plunge my searching tongue into her mouth to taste her as much as I can. Our tongues collide in a dominating battle, and I almost lose my mind and take her right here, right now, but I'm not sure she'd appreciate that.

When I pull away, I miss her soft lips within seconds and when she licks them, I want to lick them too. "Who are you?" I ask with a frown.

Where did she come from, I want to ask because it's clear she's not in her usual habitat and she clearly doesn't want to be here.

She laughs, "Hayley."

"Pleasure to meet you, Hayley. I'm Asher," I reply and hold her hand in mine, completely mesmerized by her entire being. "I don't want to steal you from your friends tonight although it's clear you don't want to be here, but you're probably doing it for a friend. But I want to take you out," I continue and kiss the palm of her tiny hand.

When she smiles sweetly, I know she'll agree. "Okay."

"Okay. Here, give me your cell number," I add and quickly grab the phone from my pocket and hand it over to her. She writes her number, her real one I hope, and she hands it back to me after she's saved it under the name 'My girl'. I smile widely. Damn right she'll be my girl and she knows it, so I hope those two guys that are in her group, and any man in this room for that matter of fact, will keep their hands to themselves or I might find myself murdering them all if they touch her in any way.

In the span of 30 minutes, I became this possessive ass, who wishes she won't ever be in the same room with any man ever again and I frown at the thoughts crossing my mind. I haven't been like this since I was 20 years old and I'm not sure how I feel about it, but for now, I'll enjoy it.

She gives me this feeling inside my chest that I haven't felt before. Like my heart is melting, or some shit, and my mother always used to say that when you see someone and you feel like you'd known them your whole life, then you have to hold on onto that because it means that in a different life, you were important to each other.

That's exactly how I feel about Hayley.

So I'm going to hold onto it.

THREE | HAYLEY

PRESENT DAY

Is he and his assistant the only thing I've been thinking for way too long for my own sanity?

Yes.

Was I wishing to be the one on that desk?

Fuck yes.

Was he right when he called me up on it? He surely was but it's out of my control. I almost wanted to pleasure myself right in the middle of the company, in my new office. That's how horny I was, and I haven't been horny in years.

I have never wanted a man to touch me like I want Ace to touch me and I'm not sure it's because of our history or just how he makes me feel now.

I've tried to have sex since I became a free young woman, but the thought of a man touching me again, sent me running before they got to open their mouths, so I gave out after a few tries.

Maybe I'm broken forever, but after all, it's just sexual pleasure and release, so my fingers work just fine.

After Sebastian's death, I thought I was free. I had hoped so, but I was so wrong, because he broke me in so many ways, that I'm not sure I'll ever be free of my demons again.

The bastard made sure of it.

He took each fear and brought it to life in the cruellest way. For three years he made sure I remained silent and loyal through each and every one of his horrors.

We reach the restaurant a few minutes later and I follow Ash around like a lost puppy, even though I try my best not to show it, I have no idea what I'm doing, but that's the point, isn't it? When I find a way to tarnish the Dawson name, I'll also bring down the company.

That's the fucking dream.

When we reach the restaurant's doors, I remember to plaster a smile back on my face and while Ash holds the door for me, I enter with my head held high. He leads me toward our table and I'm relieved to see that whoever this lady he's meeting is, hasn't arrived yet.

The restaurant is a mix of posh exterior to attract people but cozy and comfortable interior to keep them coming back.

The waiter on duty rushes over to greet us and place two menus on our table. I take the menu in complete silence and try to focus on it while being aware of Asher's close proximity.

Why is this table so fucking small?

Asher touches my shoulder to bring me back into the room and I flinch before I can stop myself. "Are you okay?" he asks with a confused look. Or is it concern? Probable none of the two. He doesn't care about me, that he made clear.

"Mhm. Yeah, just hungry," I say quickly and raise my hand to flag down our waiter, who's very quick to arrive and I'm very grateful for that. He just got himself a big tip. "I'll have a garden salad and a fresh orange juice."

Asher eyes me suspiciously because I just said I'm hungry, but I ordered a salad. It's the best I can stomach near him anyway.

"I'll have the slow-cooked salmon with an extra side of fries and a diet coke," he gives his order, closes the menu and hands it to the boy.

I look at the waiter, and then at him. Fries and salmon? That's odd. "Coke Zero's way better," I joke, and he smiles, revealing those beautiful dimples of his.

"I agree, but they don't have any," he replies, and I find myself relaxing for the first time in the last 24 hours.

God, this is a lot harder than I anticipated.

"Do you like your new office?"

I search his face for any clues of what might be going through his head, but I don't find any. "It could use some redesigning, but it'll do for now."

"Don't get too comfortable, sweetheart. You won't be there for long," he replies, and I work very hard to not let my smile falter. How the hell does this man go from laughing to a piercing gaze?

How can he act one minute like we're friends and the next like he hates my guts?

Luckily for me, the waiter returns with our

drinks and releases some of the tension that was building up. "Miss Diaz called, Mr. Dawson and apologized but she won't be able to make it to this meeting. She asked that you reschedule."

I frown. That's odd or maybe the lady just isn't interested enough in what this company has to offer.

"Sebastian had a very good relationship with this woman, but since I took over, she will always find reasons to cancel on me," he explains and I stiffen when I hear his brother's name, catching Asher's eye in an instant. He scans my face, trying to read me, but doesn't say anything.

"Maybe she doesn't like you," I say with a straight face.

"Impossible, I'm very likable, wouldn't you say?" he replies, and I burst out laughing again, and that probably surprises me more than it does him.

Our food arrives and I stare at my salad for a long time before actually picking up the fork. Asher eats his fish like a gentleman, with a knife and fork and I watch him with awe. I wish I had that kind of appetite, but I don't anymore, because Sebastian had to make sure I didn't gain any weight, so instead I lost some. I actually lost too much, and I've never managed to get it back.

When Ash catches me watching him, he puts down his knife and fork and takes a sip of his drink. "You should eat something more consistent than leaves, Hayley. You're too thin for your own good."

His comment isn't in any way mean, it's actually the most considerate he's been since this morning, but I decide to fight him anyway. "Why do you care?"

"I don't, but you're sitting at my table, in my company, so you'll eat well," he orders, and I swallow the lump in my throat.

"I can't. I used to have a very strict diet and now it's hard for me to eat carbs without feeling sick, so I just stick to leaves."

Here I am being honest again. *Why do you have to share everything, Hayley? He would never pity you, so why are you being stupid?*

"You never needed a damn diet in the first place, you looked perfect," he replies with a grimace, but it quickly seems like he regrets saying that.

I don't, it's the nicest thing someone's said to me in a very long time, and I take it like a breath of fresh air even if that means there's going to be cracks in my walls, I'm going to take that risk.

"I know," I whisper and leave it at that.

He sighs and pushes the fries toward me. "These are the healthiest and most bio-organic fries you can get, so have some. It'll help you ease into more carbs."

I think about it for a second and then reach slowly, pick up a French fry and take a bite. My mouth sensors completely drown in the salty, fried yet healthy taste of the fries. I continue to eat them with my hand, like a teenage girl, all while Ash watches me with a smile, but when I notice him, I stop.

If his words won't break my walls, that smile will definitely do it.

"What can I do to make you leave this town for good this time?" he shocks me with the question and here I was thinking we've made progress.

I push my plate and wipe away at the corners of my mouth.

If I didn't have a good appetite before, now I've completely lost it.

I throw him a pointed glare and take a sip of my orange juice. "I'm not going anywhere, Ace. Not until I've done what I came here to do, only then I can rest in peace, so you can try anything and everything that crosses your pretty mind, it won't work. I'm here to stay and this time I'm going to win."

He analyses my face with the intensity of a detective, probably trying to understand what I meant by that. He won't though, not until it'll be too late, and I would've taken his company down with me. "Now if you'll excuse me, it seems like we're done here," I say through gritted teeth and take a hundred bill out of my wallet and place it on the table.

"When did you become this shell of a woman, Hayley?" he asks with a hardened gaze when I've managed to sit up.

"When I stopped hoping that you'd come to save me from my own personal hell," I reply with a sad, broken smile and start walking toward the exit.

As soon as I step into the chilly air of Westport, I take a deep breath in and release it slowly before I spot a cab and run to flag it down.

I know exactly what I need right now and that's a glass of wine and a good book to help me forget about Asher. Or maybe a porn and some release, but who knows where this day will lead me?

This fucking town is full of surprises, so I can never be prepared enough.

HAYLEY

FOUR YEARS AGO

When I return to our table, everyone giggles and tries to hide their cheeky smiles. So, they saw me with my mysterious man. So what?

Asher.

I can't contain my smile, and everyone laughs at my expense.

"Do you even know who you just kissed?" Jennifer asks with a mischievous and slightly shocked smile. Why is she being so cryptic all of a sudden.

I raise a brow. "Correction. *He* kissed me."

"Tomaeto, tomato. That's Asher Dawson. One of the owners of this club," she giggles and tries very hard not to look his way, but when I do, he smiles at me and it's clear he knows that I know who he is now.

Am I shocked?

Heck yeah.

Am I sorry?

Fuck no.

He looks like a Greek God and he kisses like one too, although I've never kissed one before, but I've also never met anyone like Asher before.

He's mysterious, but kind. His smile is warm and mischievous, like he imagines me in different positions and that thought warms up my insides, making me clench my thighs together.

I can't say that I'm a prude, but I'm not the most open person either, so these thoughts are more than new to me.

"He asked me out," I announce with a squeal, and everyone cheers for me attracting even more attention, but I don't really care.

I almost want to jump up and down with excitement, but I have to contain it all inside until I get home. The things he made me feel with his tongue and how his hands held the back of my head will definitely help me get off later tonight.

"Daamn girl. That's asking for some dancing, let's go," she says with a stern look and stands up taking me with her. I realize I know the song that's playing because it's from one of those hot Italian actors from 365 Days.

I think it's called 'Feel it' and what surprises me even more is to learn that Asher is the one who requested to be put on, by the way he watches me laid back on his sofa with lust in his eyes.

He looks at me like he could eat me alive.

And the worst thing is, I like it.

I want it.

I crave it.

I start swaying my hips on the beats of the slow seductive song with Jennifer behind me, but I can swear he only has eyes for me because his gaze never leaves mine and the room seems to grow hotter by the minute.

I decide to tease him a little bit by turning around and grabbing Jennifer's hips in a provocative gesture. I pull her closer and she smiles seductively even though she knows that I'm using her.

She widens her eyes in surprise in the next second and when a pair of large strong palms grab my stomach and pulls me back, I almost whimper, but when his low voice whispers in my ear, I melt and become a puddle in his arms. "I thought I had to keep my eyes on the guys in the room, but I forgot that a woman could also easily steal you."

I laugh and rest my head on his shoulder, continuing to move on to the song while butterflies suddenly start playing in my stomach.

"I'm not laughing, *butterfly*, keep that one away from you, I know she's lesbian," he snarls behind me, and I roll my eyes.

"Not going to happen. She's my best friend and my roommate," I reply and turn around to face him, but I don't think that's a good idea because seeing his strong jawline now that he's upset makes dirty things happen to my sex-deprived coochie.

"I can be your roommate," he wraps his arms around me, pulling me closer, and grins at me, revealing those beautiful dimples that make me wet.

Is he serious?

He can't be serious though.

I don't even know him. What if he's a rapist and a predator?

"You're crazy, we just met," I laugh in response.

"I'm never letting you go, beautiful." Now he's definitely serious because his dimples are gone, so there's no smile.

"You're beautiful," escapes my mouth before I can stop myself.

Shit, Hayley. You're not supposed to say that to guys.

"You think so?" he teases and places a soft kiss on the tip of my nose.

I nod in response to his question and try hard to contain a yawn because his embrace and this slow song don't help my tiredness.

"Let me take you home, you don't want to be here," he observes and maybe I should be insulted that he thinks he knows what I want, but I'm not.

I'm actually relieved when I hear the word home and I realize that I really need my bed right now, so I agree to his suggestion with another nod and look around for Jen who I found dancing with a girl. I walk toward her and speak in her ear so she can hear me. "I'm going home, but don't worry. Asher will take me; you stay and have fun."

"Are you sure you don't want to stay a little while longer?" she asks.

"I really don't. I have had a horrible migraine since I walked in here." I finally tell her the truth and I know from the way a smile spreads on her lips that she doesn't believe me.

"That's what they call a boner these days?" she laughs and even though I want to correct her, I'm not in the mood for arguing even though nothing's going to happen no matter how horny I am.

I return to where I left Asher and we both exit the club. I almost want to kiss the silence but that's physically impossible, so I just release a long breath. "I'll have something for that headache in my car," he says, and I smile.

I link my arm with his and we start walking slowly in the chilly night, but I don't mind the cold because as long as he touches any part of me, I'm bound to be warm. "Asher, I'm not a one-night stand type of girl."

He stops to search my face and to whisper close to my mouth. "I could pursue you to be, but baby, when I fuck you, I need you to enjoy yourself without any headache stopping that."

I swallow hardly and feel my pussy clench at the thought of what he could do to me and my body. What I would like him to do to me.

Damn, Hayley. Who are you?

"Besides, I said I'll never let you go, remember? That was a promise, Hayley."

Fuck this headache.

He can take me right fucking now.

Right fucking here, in his spacious car. "I've got butterflies, Asher. Why are you doing this to me?" I ask and hide my face on his chest. I can't look at his face anymore because it's all too unreal for me. It's like one of my book boyfriends came to life for me.

Asher pinches my chin to lift it up. "Butterflies are good, baby. They're good," he whispers close to my lips, and when he presses his softly onto mine, my bones melt, and I lean into his warm arms.

"I don't want to go home," I whine, and he chuckles. "That can be arranged," he says and presses a button that brings down a visor between us and the driver. "James, please take us to the park. We could use a stroll," he then addresses the driver and I smile euphorically.

He could've taken my words differently and asked the driver to take us to his apartment instead, but he's being a gentleman all the way, regardless of the very big and probably painful bulge in his pants. "You're like a dream, Am I dreaming?"

"It depends, are you usually this horny in your dreams?" he whispers close to my ear, and his breath sends electricity all over my body.

I should say yes, but instead I say, "No. I'm not. You're doing this to me, and I want to be a good girl so badly. I want to say goodnight, go home and get myself off, but I can't."

Then I do something I've never done before. I reach between us and take off my panties. My eyes don't leave Asher's face for a second, and the lust written on every inch of his beautiful features brings out a moan.

Some may think I'm drunk, others may think that I'm drugged, but I am simply intoxicated by this beautiful man. He emanates masculinity through every pore, and I *need* to see how far his touch can take me.

For a second, when Asher doesn't move a muscle, I'm afraid I might've made a mistake and scared him off, but then he's so quick to grab the underwear from my hand, that I'm fazed a little. "This stays with me."

I nod in approval, and he sticks them in his pocket just before he captures my lips in another kiss. This time is different though. It's hungry and desperate and I'm here for it. I bathe in it. I let him devour me and when he reaches underneath my dress and his fingers go straight to my clit, something ignites in my brain, and I bite his lip hard.

Asher releases a deep and throaty moan. "You're a wild one, aren't you?"

The realization and gleam in his eyes bring a smile to my face. "You have met your match, Mister Dawson."

"Did I, now?" He whispers and I moan. He hasn't even touched me yet and I'm on fire. "Do you want me to touch you, wild one?"

I can't say for sure, but I think his ocean blue eyes have darkened a few shades and the fire sizzling in them makes me whimper with need. "Y-yes."

"You have to ask nicely," he retorts, and I lean into him even more. I am so close to jumping on and dry humping him that I'm afraid he'll retract his date invitation.

He wants me to ask, or even beg, but I've never done that before and I have to admit, I'm a bit reluctant to start now with a complete stranger but in the heat of the moment, who cares about dignity?

I want his touch so badly, that if he'd ask me to kneel and crawl, I probably would and I'm not even ashamed of thinking that.

FOUR | ASHER

PRESENT DAY

It's been 3 days since Hayley came back to town and I have been on edge ever since. I haven't seen her since our restaurant lunch, but I've been playing every conversation we had in my head but all that's managed to do, has only confused me even more.

She's been throwing words at me that left me analysing them and coming up with nothing. First, she said my brother was a piece of shit, which led me to ask myself if she hated him, why did they get married all of a sudden? She couldn't have been pregnant because they never had a baby or at least, not that I know of. Then she said something about everything he's done to her, so what happened?

What the hell is the real story and what did they hid from me for so long, and even worse, what is she hiding from me now?

I remember that one time I came home from London for a brief meeting, and Hayley was in Sebastian's office, waiting for him all lost in thought. Seeing her in his chair made me freeze and I couldn't move, but I remember how she took out something from her purse completely unaware that someone was watching. It was a concealer and she started tapping her left wrist with it. At the time, the gesture confused me, but now I can't stop but wonder, was she covering up a bruise?

Could it have been a bruise made by my brother?

"He chose the wrong bitch to destroy." What is that supposed to mean? How did he destroy her when she always had a smile on her face around him?

I need to get to the bottom of this or I won't be able to focus on anything else. I need to figure out what her plans are and most importantly, how to get rid of her as soon as possible.

I pick up the cell phone from my pocket and call my private investigator. "Daniel, I have some work for you. I need you to find a person and to follow another one for the time being. I need to know this woman's every move."

"You got it, boss, give me a few hours and I'll get back to you. Who am I searching for and who am I following?"

"The first one's name is Jennifer Sinclair, and she is friends with Hayley Dawson, the one I need you to follow."

"Sure thing," he replies.

I hang up the call and lean back on the sofa, resting my head on the headrest. She's been here for less than a week and I am already losing my mind.

The need to kiss her is just as intense as it's always been.

The need to touch her is driving me insane and keeps my pants tight, regardless of how many times I release the tension with my own hand, it will come to life as soon as her lips, face or body comes to mind.

When they called and told me my brother had died in a car accident, my first thought was about her.

How is she? Is she okay?

Was she in the car with him? Did she get hurt? But then I found out he was alone in the car and that his brakes failed and even though I refused to believe it, I had to accept that Hayley had done that. It had to be her, otherwise, she wouldn't have stayed home. They were supposed to go to that event together and she refused to go in the last minute.

Thinking about Jennifer, I open Google search on my phone and search up her name, surprisingly, getting only a few results in Westport. After a few checks on each website, I find her advertising her lawyer services and I smile, quickly dialling the number on the screen.

"Jennifer Sinclair, family court lawyer," she introduces herself and waits for me to speak.

"Hi, my name is Dylan O'Brien and I want to find out the process of divorce, can I book an appointment for today? Or as soon as possible?"

I met Jennifer on the same night I met Hayley because they were roommates at the time, but I'm sure she won't recognize my voice that easily.

"Of course, Mr. O'Brien. I'm in the office all day today so you can pop by at any time. I'll text you the address if that's okay with you," she replies from the other end of the line, and I release a relaxing breath because it's exactly what I needed to hear.

Great fucking news.

"Great, I'll be there in half an hour," I say before ending the call and grabbing my suit jacket.

My driver, Eddie is in the car waiting for me in front of the building as usual and I give him the address as soon as I'm in the backseat.

Her office is on the cheaper side of town, all the way across from DBSA tower and that's why I knew it'd take me 30 minutes to get there, and when we pulled up in front of her office, I realised it's been a lot quicker and hope that she's not on a lunch break or something. "I'll be quick," I say, and he laughs.

Pervert.

I walk toward Jennifer's office and open the huge door that says family court law under her name. As soon as I'm in I find a small reception with a young lady, looking to be in her early twenties.

She smiles at me widely and stands up from her desk to greet me. "You must be Mr. O'Brien. Right this way," she leads me toward Jennifer's door and knocks twice before opening it. I'm sure Jennifer recognizes me even if it's been 4 years, I haven't changed at all and when she rises from her chair with a surprised look on her face, it's definite.

"Thanks, Sarah," she dismisses her assistant.

"Asher Dawson, who would've thought. You're Dylan O'Brien?" she laughs and gestures at me to take a sit, so I do.

"I didn't want to just show up here and creep you out," I reply with a grin.

She shakes her head like she can't believe her eyes. "You are creeping me out. Why are you here if not for my lawyering?"

Good fucking question. I have no clue.

"I was surprised when you weren't at Sebastian's funeral," I say, and she looks equally amused and confused by my words.

"Why would I come to his funeral? It's not like we were friends," she frowns and leans back in her chair.

"But you were Hayley's best friend, weren't you? She had no one by her side," I say through gritted teeth, a bit too accusatory.

I didn't know I was so worried about Hayley being alone when I almost made her leave her husband's funeral.

"She *had* no one, dummy. Sebastian made sure of that as soon as they got married." My throat is dry, and I need a drink. What the fuck is that supposed to mean?

"What do you mean?" I ask in a breath.

Jennifer sighs deeply and takes a long breath before she says anything else. "Look, it's not my story to tell, but I'll tell you this. Hayley was the victim, not your brother."

"She keeps saying that, but I don't understand

what she's talking about. They always looked so happy." I share with this woman I met one time, years ago like she's my best friend.

But she seems to have answers I don't.

"That's because you were on a different continent and things are easy to fake on photos and TV. Stop blaming her for everything and make sure you hear the whole story. I just can't be the one to tell it to you. You have to find her wherever she is now and this time, listen to her, Asher. You owe her that."

I knew when I came here that there might be more behind this story, but this conversation made me even foggier than before.

"What do you mean wherever she is? She's in Westport. She's been back for a few days. She never reached out?" I ask with a frown.

If Sebastian really was this bad guy they both describe, why did she never reach out after he died? Why didn't she tell me this story they keep talking about?

"She's changed, Asher. He changed her, he fucking broke her, and you helped him!" she accuses me and I'm speechless for a very long minute. I look out the window for a few seconds, unable to look her in the eyes.

"I can't listen to this anymore, Jennifer. It's like you both talk in fucking riddles," I say and jump out of my seat.

I have to get out of here.

"They're not riddles. It's just too much history.

It's not all just black and white, Asher. Wake up!" she says from behind me, but I exit before I hear anything else.

If there's a story, I'll hear it and then I'll find out if it's real or not.

Who was my brother? Was he truly a monster or is everyone trying to play me?

ASHER

FOUR YEARS AGO

"You have to say it, Hayley. Tell me what you need, baby." Hayley melts in my arms just like any other girl, but unlike the others, I melt for her too. She craves my touch, but she's too innocent to ask for it, so it's my pleasure to take that innocence.

Her black dress is hiked up and my palm touches the soft skin of her thighs, making her want more, but denying it until she learns to ask for it. It's not that I like to make women beg for it, but more about wanting Hayley to unleash her sexual energy.

"Please, Asher. I need your touch," she leans in and whispers in my ear. Her warm breath caresses my ear, and a jolt runs straight to my groin.

I smile, and ignoring the growing pain between my own legs, I reach down and touch her exactly where she burns hotter.

When I start rubbing her clit, she bites my neck.

When I insert two fingers, she bites my ear and releases a breathy moan. "What are you doing to me, Asher?"

"Only pleasurable things, I hope," I reply with a grin and intensify my finger thrusts. "You like it, baby?"

"Yes. Yes. Don't stop, Asher. Don't stop," she pleads and starts riding my fingers.

"Never. Not even if the world ends around us. Ride it, baby. I can't wait to taste your cum on my fingers."

A few seconds later when she starts shaking and moaning, I know she's reached the sweet climax. I let her collapse on my side and hold her with my left arm while I still have my fingers deep inside of her.

A few moments pass before I release my fingers and she gets more comfortable at my side. I open my mouth to say something, but I realise that her breathing slowed, and she's fallen asleep.

I smile and continue to hold her quietly, while I text my driver to take us to her apartment and when we reach it, I let him get a cab and go home.

She looks so peacefully sleeping, without a care in the world, like she's not next to a stranger. Good thing I'm a good guy, I guess.

I close my eyes for a minute and when I open them later, it looks like the sun is coming up. I snap my head to my right, where I left Hayley sleeping and find her wide awake.

"Morning, handsome," she whispers with a smile.

"I fell asleep," I say almost in shock.

"We both did. Wanna come upstairs for a coffee? I think I owe you that much," she offers with a shy smile that I find beyond adorable.

I don't ever want to leave her side, so if she wants me here, here I'll stay.

"Sure," I accept and we both head for the apartment.

When we enter the small apartment, I'm actually surprised by the way it's decorated and how clean it is.

"Don't look too grossed out by the size of this place. I know you've never seen a palace before, but this is a palace, so get used to it," she scolds me, and I follow her in with a full-hearted laughter.

She takes off her jacket and turns the coffee machine on. "What's your poison?"

Definitely not coffee, but she can't know that, so I ask for something with more milk than coffee. "I don't know, a latte. More milk, less coffee."

She tilts her head to the side. "You don't actually drink coffee, do you?"

"I don't, but I couldn't pass on the offer to see this palace, could I?" I joke and lean on the kitchen counter.

My God, she's beautiful.

***

She promised me a date, but it's been almost a week and she barely replies to my texts. Today is finally Friday so I'm hoping now that college is finished for the week, she'll finally go out with me.

Today I choose not to call or text, so before I

reach her College, I grab a bouquet of red roses and continue on my way to the gates. I coerced her roommate Jennifer into telling me what time they finish so I didn't miss her, so here I am at 8 pm, on a chilly October evening.

When she sees me, the look on her face makes this long and agonizing week all worth it. I greet her with a wide grin, and she strolls over like she doesn't want to jump in my arms, barely containing her happiness. "I'm an asshole, I'm sorry. I just had too many exams this week and didn't think you'd care enough for me to whine at you," she explains when she stops a few steps from me.

Shaking my head, I pull her into my arms and kiss the lips I've been literally dreaming about all week. They're a lot softer than I remember and I want the feel of them to be embedded in my brain, so I never lose the memory.

She relaxes in my arms and wraps her own around my neck to pull me closer and deeper in the kiss.

I think I'm fucking addicted.

"The thought of you not wanting me terrified me, and no woman has ever terrified me before, in any way. Now, how about that date you promised me?" I whisper low in my throat and keep her wrapped in my arms.

It's the second time I see her and maybe I shouldn't have said that, but she smiles in reply.

"Will I get away with you maybe letting me go

change first?"

She knows the answer to her question before I utter the words. "You look fantastic, and you smell divine, so no. Not when there's no need for that."

I hold out a hand for her and when she takes it with a smile, I squeeze her slightly and lead her to my car, where my driver James waits for us.

We both climb onto the back seat and when Hayley sits on the opposite side of the car, I growl and pull her into my arms giving her no choice but to straddle me. Her skirt climbs up on her hips leaving her pussy protected by a piece of underwear only, and that thought makes me lose my mind. "The things I wanna do to you, Hayley... I'm not sure you'd still want me afterward," I whisper on her soft skin, and she shivers in my arms in response. I pull her face closer to mine and kiss her lips with hunger.

I can feel her thighs clenching around me and my dick twitches. "Baby, you have to stop that or I'm going to come in my pants like a teenage boy," I breathe the words and avoid moving my hips at all.

"I want you just as much, Ace," she surprises me with her admission and with the nickname she uses but when she rolls her hips slightly, I forget how to breathe altogether.

"Damn it, baby, I can't take you here, no matter how much I want it," I breathe the words and thrust my hips forward, making her moan in return.

God, we're lucky James can't see or hear

anything, or I'd have to kill him.

Hayley continues to move her hips in rolling motions, and I almost lose my mind. Our breathing becomes labored, and her moans intensify, meaning she's close to her release. I grab her hips in my palms to help her with her motion because I know she's getting tired.

She closes her eyes tightly and bites her bottom lip, but all I can do is watch her face as she gets close to coming undone. "Eyes on me, baby," I growl and tighten my grip on her waist. She opens her eyes wide. "I need your eyes on me when I make you come," I add between clenched teeth and immediately feel Hayley's body shattering on top of me.

When I'm done staring at her euphoric face, I realize we have arrived at the DBSA tower, and where my penthouse is.

"Look at what a mess you've made of my pants, sweetheart," I say under my breath, and even in the low-lit car, I can tell she's blushing.

"I'm sorry."

"Don't be. It's the most arousing thing you could do."

"I've never, hmm," she clears her throat but doesn't finish the sentence.

"You've never what, baby?"

"I've never had an orgasm before that wasn't provoked by my fingers, and you've already given me two," she whispers so low that I can barely hear her but when I finally understand what she's saying, I smile.

"Oh baby, but this was hardly an orgasm provoked by me. I'll have to show you how that really feels."

We exit the car and I have to hold her because it seems like she won't be able to be steady on her feet after the orgasm she had. I still have a boner, but I'm lucky it's covered by my long wool coat.

"What are we doing here? Isn't this like an office building?" she asks as we enter the huge building. I greet Simon, who's working the reception tonight.

"It is, but it's also where I live," I reply.

She frowns but lets me lead her toward the elevator anyway.

She doesn't say anything else until the elevator stops and opens in my penthouse. I hope she won't run away before I get a chance to explain that I didn't bring her up here for sex. She gasps and is frozen in place when she sees my fully windowed living room.

"Did I fall asleep and miss our date?" she asks, and a chuckle escapes me before I can stop myself.

I love her sarcasm.

"No, baby, of course not. Be patient," I say as I lead her outside, toward the patio area.

I can't tell if she's disappointed or just shocked.

FIVE | HAYLEY

PRESENT DAY

When I arrived back in Westport, I got this crazy idea that I should look for my birthmother, so I did. I lived here my entire life, so that means she must've too, but when I went to the orphanage I was left at, they couldn't help me much, other than giving me a name.

Samantha Banks.

I've been searching this name on every social media app and on Google for a few days, until last night, I think I found someone whom my gut tells me it might be her, but the problem is, now I don't know what to do with the information, so I decide I need a strong coffee and a soft croissant to get my day started and think this through.

I don't have many places that I like in Westport, but the Cafe called Dark Beans, next to my old College campus is definitely a place I missed.

I enter the small place with a nostalgic smile on my face but as soon as the door closes behind me, I almost turn around and run out of the shop because staring at me is a person I didn't think I'd see anytime soon, or I'd hoped so, because I always knew she stayed in town.

"Jen," I whisper with a lump in my throat. I can't cry. I can't let that door slip open or the dam might swallow me whole.

She doesn't seem to have the same problem because my best friend's cheeks are streaming with tears and before I have to decide and react in some way, she runs toward me and wraps her arms around me. "You're here," I whisper on her shoulder.

"Of course, I'm here. I've been coming here almost every day for 3 years, hoping I'd get to see you," she sniffles and wipes at her eyes.

Her words shock me to the core, and I don't think I can hold myself together anymore.

"You did?" I whisper again, and she leads me toward our secluded corner.

"Oh, sweetie, I missed you so much," she replies with a nostalgic smile and holds my hands into hers after we sit down in front of each other.

A tear escapes from my right eye but I wipe it before it gets to roll off my cheek.

"How did you know I was back?" I ask.

Jennifer looks like she weighs whether or not to tell me and I think I know it before she says it. "Asher came to see me."

As soon as she confirms my fear, I feel the world crumbling beneath my feet and my throat goes dry and constricted. "Oh no, Jennifer, what did you tell him? What did he ask you?"

She shakes her head before I get to spiral down with worry. "Nothing. I swear, but babe, what could I tell him? I don't know much myself besides the fact that Sebastian was the devil."

A bitter smile pulls at my lips. "He was so much more than that, Jennifer. He was an undiscovered type of psychopath and I used to wonder if his obsession was stemmed from knowing that I actually loved his brother and would never love him."

I tell my best friend and the next breath I take feels so lightweight that I could cry in relief. God, I haven't felt like this in what feels like ages.

"I never liked that man, but Hayley, you married him so quickly, what happened? How did he convince you?" she asks with a concerned tone, and I find myself wanting to share everything with her. Because when I'm done, I know she won't stop me from going through with my plan.

"He didn't convince me, Jen. He forced me. That's why I could never tell Ash the truth because after I had that amazing few weeks with him, his brother raped me and taped parts of it, so he threatened to show Ash what a whore I was, just before he killed him. He swore he'd kill Ash before I got a word out, so I didn't know what to do. I had no one to look at for help, no one to help me fight him."

Jennifer is so shocked that she remains silent for many minutes. I'm not even sure she's breathing anymore but, in all honesty, neither am I.

I've never spoken my truth out loud and I have no idea how to react.

"I... Hayley, you've been through this all by yourself..." It was, and it wasn't a question at the same time because she knew that besides her, I had no one else, and he made me cut any contact with her.

"So now you know why I can't tell Asher any of it yet because he's a Dawson. He'll always be a Dawson even if it hurts to be around him and not being able to tell him everything or ask him to hold me. I want him to hold me so fucking bad, but I can't. I can't let myself feel again or everything might catch up with me. I'm afraid that if I open that gate, it'll flood my mind, my body, and my soul and I don't know if I'll ever recover from it. I need everyone to learn what a piece of shit Sebastian Dawson was first and then I don't care what happens to me after that."

Jennifer takes a deep breath and from the look on her face, I can tell she's processing all the information I've given her. It's a lot to take in and digest.

"Don't say that. He doesn't deserve your pain from beyond the grave. How can I help?" she surprises me with her question, and I stare at her for a long minute. Asher's words ring in my head again. *'A shell of a woman.'*

"You're doing enough already, trust me," I whisper.

"I'm here for you, Hayley. I'm here now, so don't do this by yourself. You don't have to anymore. I can help, I want to help. If the bastard wasn't dead,

I would've killed him with my bare hands for what he did to you."

On the brick of breaking down, I realise that I have to go before that happens. I cannot let that happen under any circumstance, at least not yet.

We exchange numbers and I leave the cafe with wobbly legs. When I arrive outside, I steady myself by putting a hand on the wall and take a few deep breaths in.

This was not how I saw my day going and I think it'll get worse if Ash decides to come around asking more questions, so I head towards the one place I'm looking forward to go to, a therapist's office.

When I reached out to better help yesterday, I wasn't sure what to expect from them, because I don't think anyone can compare with my old therapist Samantha, but being miles apart, means I need a new one, so here I am, in one of their therapist's room. When I left Westport, I found refuge and friendship in my therapist and therapy might be the answer again.

"Miss Marshall, my name is Cinthya, it's so nice to meet you. Thank you for taking the time to reach out, please have a seat." She gestures toward the sofa in the corner of the comfy room, and I sit down with an awkward smile on my face. Yes, I've done this before, but it doesn't mean it gets easier pouring your life experiences onto a stranger.

"Thank you, Cinthya. Please call me Hayley," I whisper and I'm sure my smile is sad because she mimics it with one of her own.

"No problem, Hayley. Before we start this session there's a few important things I have to make you aware of such as how everything you share with me will always be confidential unless I think you or others might be at risk of harm. Our sessions have to be on a weekly basis in order for this to help and it'll always be on the same day and at the same time. Do you have any questions so far?"

I shake my head.

"Okay. Sure. There's more in the contract they've emailed over and if you have any questions we can discuss them next week, does that sound good?" she asks, and I nod. "What brings you in to see me today, Hayley?"

I think about the day I spent with Asher and how he went from telling me I need more food, because I look unhealthy, to trying to get rid of me. "Hope. Hope brought me here today because I realised how dangerous hope can be."

"What do you mean by that?" she asks with a serious face.

I sigh and take a pillow to place it on my lap, and I reply without making eye contact. "I had lunch with a ghost from my past a few days ago, and I felt normal. I felt like we were making progress until he asked me what he could do to make me leave the town."

"What would make him ask you that?"

"The things he thinks I did," I say without worry. That's the beauty of therapy. You can say almost anything and be sure that no one close will ever hear it.

"What would some of those things be, if you feel like you can speak about it," she urges me to unpack my trauma.

I almost want to laugh but I stop myself. "I'll never be brave enough to share with anyone how I went from being in love to wanting to die in the span of 24 hours."

HAYLEY

FOUR YEARS AGO

I don't know how to answer his question, because he seems too excited for me to be here. But it's his home, his personal space, and in a way, it does feel like he is sharing a piece of himself with me this way. It's one step before meeting his parents' kind of thing, and I'm not afraid or disappointed to be here, it's just that I know what he thought about when he planned to bring me here. Or maybe he signalled his driver in some way when things got heated up between us?

He places a hand on the small of my back and leads me to a set of stairs. Is he taking me to his bedroom already?

I should've known that a man like Asher would never want anything else from me than sex. It's what they're best at.

When we're on the second floor, I see he's leading me toward the outdoor patio where there's a pool, a jacuzzi, some loungers, and garden furniture. When we step onto the wooden deck, I also see the candlelit picnic he's got ready for us on our left and my heart swells in my chest.

This is so much more thoughtful than a fancy

dinner reservation at some high-end restaurant and he did it all for me. The whole terrace is wrapped in fairy lights making it magical. My eyes fill up with tears before I can stop them, and Asher quickly grabs my face into his huge palms and presses a soft kiss onto my lips. "Don't you dare cry. I never want to see you cry, baby," he whispers on my lips, and I nod.

We walk in silence toward the comfortable setting and after I lose my coat and he does the same, we sit on the pillows. There's food, fruit, cheese, snacks, and wine and I feel like my heart could burst any minute from the way his gaze never leaves my face.

"I'm sorry I misjudged you," I whisper and reach for his hand. He takes mine to his lips and places a soft kiss on my fingertips, sending electricity down my spine.

"It's okay, it happens a lot. The difference is, this time I truly care," he says slowly and looks at me with intensity.

I want to ask why me, but I don't.

Could I truly be so lucky?

I hope so because I'm falling for this guy and can't afford to wake up tomorrow and realize that it was all a sick game.

He motions me with his hand to turn around and hugs me from behind. His body is warm behind mine, and I close my eyes when he wraps a blanket around us.

Truth be told, I don't need a blanket to keep me

warm, because having him so close and feeling his slow breathing on my neck heats up every inch of my body. "Tonight is one of the few nights where the sky is so full of stars that you can barely see in between them."

"That sounds beautiful," I whisper.

"You're beautiful," he rasps.

I close my eyes.

Only now I realize there's music playing in the background and it's another song I like and enjoy. Crazy in love, Sofia Karlberg's version sounds softly around us and sets an unprecedented mood for me. I love a good playlist in the bedroom, but I never got to actually have one with any of the guys I've been with. They were too quick to finish before I could even properly undress.

"Asher, stop, you're making me blush."

He laughs and turns my head to the side so he can get access to my mouth. He kisses my jawline first and somehow that turns me on even more.

"I feel like I've known you forever, Hayley, yet I know nothing about you," he breathes, and I let out a silent moan.

"There's really nothing to know. I'm very boring," I reply in a strained whisper.

"I have to argue with you on that, baby because you are anything but boring. Your eyes sparkle brighter than the stars right now, and your lips make me wish I could kiss them forever," he whispers and slowly reaches toward my belly button and under my skirt. The fabric of my panties is the only thing standing between his hand and my aching core.

"Asher..." I whisper moan and push my hips forward to meet his hand even though he doesn't touch me.

"Can I touch you, baby? Can I touch you and make love to you tonight, Hayley?" he asks like the gentleman he is and he leaves my back, making me miss his heat, just to come in between my legs.

"Yes, please, please. God, yes," I say. Seeing him on his knees makes me lose my goddamned mind and all I want is for him to touch me.

He helps me get rid of my skirt and then quickly pulls down my panties having me completely naked from the waist down and inches from his face. Oh God, this would be completely mortifying if I wasn't so aroused by the look of lust on his face. Am I imagining things tonight or is he actually salivating?

He hasn't removed a single clothing item and somehow, I don't want him to. I want him to take me like we're on the run.

"I'm gonna taste you now, baby. Can I do that?" he asks with a husky voice, and I nod my head. When his tongue makes contact with my clit, a loud gasp escapes from my lips. "Baby, you're dripping wet for me," he says and dips two fingers inside of me, finding a sensitive spot that I didn't even know existed.

My heart beats fast in my chest and I'm afraid it might explode any minute. I buck my hips, basically riding his mouth exactly when Halsey's song, Not Afraid Anymore reaches the part that in combination with Asher ignites my entire body. He growls and it vibrates through me, bringing me on the brick of desperation. "I need you inside of me, Asher. Please."

He obeys my plea, and his mouth leaves my core so he can grant my wishes. He quickly unbuckles his belt and I help take out the engorged cock that I'm not even sure will fit inside me. He proceeds to take off his shirt so fast that I have to say I'm impressed.

"I want you raw, Hayley. Can I trust you baby?"

I nod. "I'm clean, I promise. Haven't been with someone in over a year and I'm on the pill.

Asher takes his place between my legs and kisses my lips once more. He holds his cock in his hand and guides it at my entrance, brushing my swollen clit and sending waves of sweet pleasure through my entire body. One movement later and the tip is inside of me, making both of us moan in unison.

My skin is buzzing, my core is throbbing, and my body is on literal fire when Asher bottoms out, making me moan loudly. His eyes squeeze shut as he starts pumping, lost in the feeling.

"You fit so well around me, baby." He groans and thrusts me with a few slow deliberate movements only to pick up the pace afterward, drawing out my orgasm.

I don't know if I have my eyes open and see the stars or if they're closed, and I see sparkles when the orgasm rolls through me like a shockwave. I ride it out with moans and pleas and Asher follows in my footsteps with low grunts and groans for his own release, making his cock twitch deep inside of me. I've never felt this before, and I never want him to stop.

I want to do this 24 hours a day.

He lays his forehead on top of mine, and we just stay there for a long minute before he manages to pull out and lie next to me breathless.

We don't say anything. We just tangle our fingers together, pull the cover on top of us and while he kisses my fingertips, I watch the stars and when one of them falls from the sky, I wish this would never end.

SIX | ASHER

PRESENT DAY

Seeing Hayley has created more confusion than answered questions and that's because I don't know what to believe anymore.

Sebastian was 10 years older than me, and I always idolized him and saw him as a God. I wanted to walk in his footsteps and make him proud every step of the way, so when he married my girlfriend, I didn't for one-second think that he could be to blame. That he could've done that on purpose.

She wants me to listen to her friend. Then that's what I'm going to do but I have some things to say too.

It's almost 4 pm and she still hasn't come to the office, so I don't have another choice but to pay her a visit. I know where she lives, what she does, and who she meets from Daniel, my PI, therefore I know she met Jennifer in a cafe yesterday and that she went to a Therapy office afterward.

I jump in the back of my car and tell Eddie where to take me, while I get lost in thoughts. I have so many questions that it might make my head explode. I need to get to the bottom of this or my fucking heart will explode. I thought she chose him. I thought she betrayed me and threw away my feelings for money, but now to find out that it might've never been her choice?

We get to her apartment building faster than I would've liked because now that I'm here, I'm not sure what I'm going to do or say. I keep asking her to leave this town when my heart screams in my chest.

I get out of the car and head toward her apartment door. I find it easily on the first floor and knock a few times before I hear some noise from inside.

I don't know why I've been expecting to be greeted by the same composed, well-dressed woman that's been roaming the office, because that's not what happens. When the door opens, Hayley's appearance takes me right back to when she was mine. Her blond hair is in a messy long braid and pulled over her shoulder and I can't stop but notice that the end reaches just beneath her breast. When her eyes meet mine, she lets out a gasp that her mouth forms with a perfect o and I get all these unholy ideas in my head, so I have to gulp down the need to say those ideas out loud and focus on what she's wearing instead. She wears an old, oversized t-shirt that hangs on one shoulder because she's too tiny to hold it at both sides and it's so long that it hangs low on her hips, but as much as I'd like to see those long legs of hers, she wears a pair of black leggings. My trail of admiration is cut short when from the apartment Milo, my marketing coordinator emerges, and I feel how my blood starts to boil in my veins. I see red for a few seconds and have to clench my jaw painfully to control my rage before I do something I'll regret. Why the fuck is this guy in her apartment?

"Asher, what are you doing here?" she comes into view next and probably senses the tension because she looks worried.

"I wanted to talk to you, but it looks like you're busy," I growl and I'm sure Milo is wondering why I am being so possessive right now but fuck me sideways if I can contain it.

"Milo was just leaving. Thanks for your services, Milo," she says to the man, and I feel the air rushing out of me like I've been punched in the gut.

"Services? What the fuck is that supposed to mean?" I grit out as soon as Milo is out of view.

"Since when do you care, Ace?" she asks me with a narrowed gaze and turns around to go inside the apartment. "I'm pretty sure you shouldn't be here anyway." I follow her and close the door behind me.

"I have questions and this time, you're going to answer them, Hayley," I say, and when she turns to confront me,

"I don't owe you anything!" she snarls and takes a calculated step toward me, but I'm 6'5 and she's 5'5 so the advantage is that I tower over her by far.

"The fuck you don't! You owe me fucking

answers. It starts to feel like you've kept me in the dark for too long, Hayley," I shout in her face and watch those lips open in surprise, and I swear that motion alone is enough to send the blood rushing to my groin, almost making me moan. I close my eyes for a second to clear my head in order to be able to get what I came here for. "You were supposed to be in the car with him when he died, so why weren't you?"

It's clear my question does something to her because her entire face changes. "How do you know that?" she asks with a cracked voice.

I shake my head in disbelief and take a step back to put some space between us or else I might do something stupid. "So, it's fucking true. Why did you cancel last minute, Hayley?" I shout again and she flinches at my sudden outburst.

She starts shaking her head in denial and starts walking backward slowly. Tears start streaming down her thin face and I almost run to take her in my arms, but I don't. I stop myself before it's too late.

The way she's acting concerns me and when her back hits the wall, she slides down and hugs her tiny body like a child and I swear, it fucking breaks my heart. The image she portrays fucks with me in ways I never knew existed and I feel this tug at my heart that leaves me speechless. "Hayley?" I manage to whisper and take only a step forward, but I stop because I don't even register what's happening.

She doesn't speak, she doesn't look at me and she doesn't stop crying. Her breathing becomes labored and it starts to look like she's struggling to breathe, and that's when I don't walk toward her, I run to her and get on my knees in front of her. "Hayley, what's wrong?" I ask when it's clear something's off. "Are you having a panic attack?" I add and she takes a shaking hand to her fast-beating heart.

I take her face in my palms and knowing that I have to distract her, I smash my lips onto her with the strength of a tsunami and as much as I want to, I can't contain a groan that escapes between my pressed lips onto hers.

Like coming back to life, Hayley's eyes snap to mine and widen in surprise but I don't let her go just yet. I take everything she has to offer and invade her mouth with my searching tongue and when she sticks her tongue in my mouth, I moan in surprise and slide my arms down her thin body until I reach her hips and lift her off the ground with ease. She quickly wraps her legs around my waist, and I stride toward the sofa, where I lay her down without breaking the kiss.

I kiss her long and slow and suddenly she reaches at my belt, setting my body on fire. However, my brain doesn't want to switch off and I can't stop the questions forming in my head. What if she's playing me just so she can evade answering my questions?

I place my hand on top of hers on the belt to stop her, pull away from the kiss, and look into her hazel eyes. I take a long steadying breath before I can speak with a strained husky voice. "We can continue this only if you answer one question. Did you fake your panic attack?"

Surprise and hurt flash in her eyes and she scoots away from my embrace. "Get out," she whispers and looks away from me.

"Hayley, I need to understand this. I need to understand all of it, please," I beg her, but this only infuriates her even more.

"Get out, now!" she shouts and points at the door with tears in her eyes.

I nod biting the inside of my cheek and stalk toward the door without saying anything else.

I don't know what to say or believe anymore.

ASHER

FOUR YEARS AGO

We lie here naked, and I find myself wishing that it'll never end. I don't want the morning to come because then I have to be responsible and not kidnap her for the entire weekend and keep her in my arms the entire time.

"Penny for your thoughts?" she whispers, and I smile.

"Was debating keeping you here for the entire weekend. A penny for yours?"

She chuckles and kisses the palm of my hand, making me shiver.

"Was wondering how a foster girl from California got so lucky, that the most wanted bachelor Asher Dawson wants to spend time with her," she replies with a sad tone and continues to play with my gigantic hand.

I chuckle at the title she used for me, but don't correct her. It is accurate. That's the name media plasters next to both me and my brother Sebastian just because we're not family men yet. "So you've searched my name online."

"Honestly, I shouldn't have. I regretted it the minute I did it. There are too many pictures of you with a different model every weekend." My smile falters, but I try to play it cool.

It's true, and not so true. Since College when I used to play soccer, having a girl around my arm was something usual, and it became a bad habit. When they started throwing themselves at me because of my name and my bank account, I gained another bad habit, sleeping with them and never calling them back.

"It's not luck, baby. It's faith. Forget about those pictures and what was before you. I swear it on my life that I'll never have eyes for another woman. I'll confess something to you. I wasn't supposed to be there that night. My brother, Sebastian was supposed to have a meeting, but he couldn't make it from London, so I had to replace him. I'm not really into that club, that was his idea and I help out sometimes."

I'm not one to believe in this type of thing, but there has to be some cosmic force involved in our meeting because I'm just too smitten to have just happened randomly.

She's like the perfect woman I never knew I dreamt about.

"I wasn't supposed to be there either. Jennifer won some kind of promotion you had running on Instagram and got a free table. We had reservations to Sapphire, and we considered until the last minute if this was a scam and maybe we should've gone there instead," she shares her part of the story and I'm honestly shocked.

I kiss the top of her head.

Now I'm sure it was faith.

"What do you study?" I ask her, trying to get to know her better.

"Me and Jennifer, we both study law. She will be a divorce and family lawyer, but I haven't decided yet. My bar exam isn't until July anyway. Do you have any other siblings besides Sebastian? I don't know much about the Dawson's, sorry."

I lift her chin to make her look me in the eye when she averts her gaze. She has no idea that the fact that she doesn't know much about me is the best thing that could happen to me.

"You don't need to apologize. I'm glad you don't know me and to answer your question, no. It's just me and Sebastian, and he's 10 years older than me. Our father died 5 years ago and left us the company on an equal split, but I don't get as involved as Sebastian because it's not my passion, and I'm sure he prefers it like that. We're half-brothers anyway." I explain and her face lights up.

"What is your passion?"

The answer comes to mind in a matter of seconds and that speaks volumes.

"I always wanted to be a firefighter, but life didn't let me. My father didn't let me."

"A millionaire firefighter, that's new," she smiles, and I can see her picturing me in that gear. That would be hot as hell.

"I'd give it all away in a second just to live a normal life, Hayley."

She frowns.

"What's stopping you?"

"Deathbed promises. My entire life I felt like I let my father down because I wanted to be a different person than he had hoped for and before he passed, he made me promise I won't leave my brother alone and we will continue the Dawson legacy."

My brother has always been the perfect son and it's always been so hard to follow his footsteps when the interests we have are so different. As soon as he began understanding business and money, Seb started following my father to the office.

At first it seemed like he just wanted to spend more time with dad, because he was never home, but then I started to see things differently. He liked being the favorite. He thrives on it.

Hayley stands upright and wraps the blanket around her before taking my face into her tiny palms.

"Asher, your father is gone, and he shouldn't dictate how you live your life from beyond the grave, it's not fair," she whispers and gets halfway up to look me in the eyes.

"It's a lot more complicated than that," I whisper and blow out a breath.

"I understand."

"I know."

I want nothing more than to show her off to the entire world and make sure that everyone know that she is mine, so I'll start with my family. "I'm having dinner with Sebastian and my mother next Saturday, and I'd like you to join us."

"I'd love that, Asher." She replies with an honest smile.

SEVEN | HAYLEY

PRESENT DAY

It's been a few hours since Asher left my apartment and I know that because now this whole place is dark and scary, but I couldn't get off the floor. I'm still on the cold floor, back at the door since he left, mind scattered everywhere. I almost let him have me, I almost trusted him again, seconds before he questioned my mental health.

I almost fell for his sweet kisses and soft whispers until his brutal question brought me back to reality. He's not the same man I fell in love with. He's not the same man who loved and protected me for a brief time.

I haven't been able to let a man touch me again because of Sebastian's abuse and when my body and my mind are in sync for once, allowing me to enjoy a man's touch, it happens for this asshole who hates me with everything he's got.

"Hayley? Are you in there?" I hear from behind the door after two soft knocks. It sounds like Jennifer, but I can't be sure. I also can't respond because my body is numb and refuses to cooperate.

"Hayley? I need to know you're okay," she speaks again and continues to knock.

I take a deep breath in. "I'm here, I'm okay, Jen. Please go."

"I'm not going anywhere, Hayley. I'm not abandoning you again, so you better open this door before I call the fire department to break it down for me," she says with a stern voice, and I think about it for a long minute. Knowing Jennifer, she'll do it for sure, so I force some strength in my body and get off the floor.

When I manage to stand up, I turn the lights on, unlock the door, and open it wide for Jennifer to come in. "I told you, I'm fine."

"You don't look fine, Hayley, what happened?" she asks while I slowly lead her to the sofa.

I sigh and nod before answering. "Asher happened. He was here."

"Oh, sweetie. What did he do now?" she asks with a frown.

"He made me come alive with a kiss, and then he killed any hope I might've had growing in the depths of my frozen heart with a question."

I never thought I'd get to speak my truth to someone other than my therapist and to say this out loud, it's like a breath of fresh air, leaving me lighter and lighter.

"Hayley..."

I wipe away the tears in the corner of my eyes and take another deep breath. "You know what I need right now? To get wasted, like in the old days. Yeah, we should do that. I should find a man and make sure he fucks me into forgetting the big brute that crushed my heart."

Jen narrows her blue eyes at me. I'm sure she's worried about my sudden mood change but honestly, so am I. Tomorrow I can get back to making plans and plotting about destroying the Dawson name, but right now, I need to take my mind off things. I need to forget that damn kiss, and how it ignited my entire body.

"If that's what you want, then I'll be there to make sure you're safe this time," she replies after a while.

I nod and give her a weak smile, before rising on my feet. "I'll go shower and you can pick something for me to wear in the meantime."

"Can I borrow a dress? I don't feel like going out in jeans today," she jokes, and I laugh then nod in approval and understanding before heading for that hot shower, that sounds great to get me out of this heavy mood.

"What did he ask you?" she shouts from my dressing room, and I think twice if I should tell her or not.

"He asked why I wasn't in the car with Sebastian the night he died." I answer honestly and I can almost hear her next question. 'Why weren't you?' but I'm left dumbfounded when it doesn't come.

"I would've helped you run; you know? I would've killed Sebastian myself if I knew, Hayley, you should've told me," She now stands in the doorway, looking at my thin body.

There are so many things I could've done

differently, but I was young and scared. I loved Asher so much, that I sacrificed myself for him.

"You really think revenge will free you, Hayley?"

I sigh deeply. "It's not revenge I'm seeking, Jen. It's redemption. This is my way of taking back control that's been stolen from me. Control that's been stolen from every single abused woman from America by every man just like Sebastian that's out there."

Jen's smile is sad, but so is mine.

HAYLEY

FOUR YEARS AGO

Asher Dawson is every woman's dream, and I am the luckiest one alive. He treats me like a queen, worships me in bed, and gives me the space I need for College. He's 6 years older than me but I swear I'll never be able to even look at a younger man because Asher showed me a different side that I didn't know men had.

We've known each other for only a few weeks now but I can say with the hand of my heart, that this man has my whole damn heart and that I'm falling for him with each passing minute that we spend together.

Although I was supposed to work last weekend, I ended up spending the entire weekend at Asher's penthouse, cuddled, worshiped and fucked into oblivion. This weekend I'm sure it'll be no different as soon as we leave the family dinner.

I have to admit that I'm nervous as hell and it took me hours to find something to wear, just because Asher's mom is not very public, and I don't know why I have a feeling she won't like me very much.

"You have to relax a bit, you look like you're

going to your own funeral," Jennifer tries to joke, but she isn't helping me at all, so I throw my stress ball at her head. "Okay, I'm just joking. But honestly, it's sweet that he wants you to meet his family so soon. He's a real Prince Charming."

I bite my bottom lip. "That's exactly why I'm so nervous, Jen. What if they don't like me and he has to choose?" I start ranting and I know it, but I can't stop myself. I'm extremely nervous and I'm usually quite a confident person.

Before I can get even more lost in my own worries, a knock sounds from the front door and Jen opens it for me. Ash strides inside in his expensive suit and smiles widely when his eyes meet mine. "Hey beautiful. Jen," he greets my friend and returns his gaze on me a second later. He runs his gaze from head to toe and back and his eyes narrow, leaving me confused. "Baby, you are so beautiful and I'm the luckiest man alive to be able to call you mine, so why did you felt like you had to dress some other way to impress my family?" He says in regard to my ankle length skirt and dark bleu blouse.

"I just want them to like me," I whisper, and he grabs my waist to pull me closer.

"I want that too, baby, but I want them to like you for who you are, not for someone you pretend to be. And if they somehow don't, then it's their loss."

His words leave me open-mouthed and I feel tears prickling at my eyes, so I have to blink them away.

"Ah, if you don't marry him, I will," Jennifer's voice sounds from a corner and I even forgot she was still in the room with us, but she isn't wrong. He is dreamy.

"I'll go change if you don't mind waiting," I say and take a step back to run towards my dressing room.

He gives me the most heart-warming smile and the butterflies come alive at the sight of those dimples. "Take all the time you need."

I run toward my room with Jennifer close behind me. "Goddamn it, woman. He's even dreamier than I remember."

"Shhh," I chuckle as we enter my room.

"What? He's probably very aware of the way he looks."

My smile is getting bigger and bigger with each passing second. "Exactly why there's this tickling feeling deep in my brain telling me that I can't be this lucky to catch the attention of... *him*."

"That's where you're wrong. You, my friend, are gorgeous and he's the one lucky to have caught your attention."

"I am a catch, aren't I?" I say a bit more confidently while I put on a knee length, hourglass shaped dress. "Okay, I'm going now. Wish me luck."

She waves a hand at me in dismissal. "You don't need any luck. They're going to love you."

"I love you," I kiss her cheek and run out to my

waiting boyfriend.

He's my boyfriend, isn't he?

"Now, that's more like it. Ready?" He asks and places a sweet kiss on my left cheek.

I nod and after I grab my long jacket from the hanger, we head out the door. "I'm so nervous, Asher."

He grabs my hand and leads me toward the elevator. "Don't be. I don't care if they like you or not. I do and that's all that matters."

I don't know who to be grateful to for what's happening now, because I'm not much of a God lover, but I believe this is the first time in 24 years that I feel the need to thank some deity for my fortune.

***

The dinner is held at their mom's house, which seems to be on the outskirts of the town and from what Asher's told me, she tries to bring everyone together for at least a dinner a month.

Asher chose to drive tonight because he wants to take me somewhere afterwards, so when the car stops, I realize he's waiting for the gates to a mansion to open while I stare at the bulging muscles on his arm with each manoeuvre he makes while shifting gears.

I think watching him drive has become my second favorite thing. I think we all agree on what the first favorite thing is.

"You look lost in thought, and I'm more than

curious to know what you're thinking about," he brings me out of my daydreaming.

I chuckle and bit ethe inside of my cheek. "You. You occupy my every thought."

"Good."

A few minutes later he parks the car and we both exit and head toward the door.

Although the setting and the drive here made me believe we are headed for a huge compound, I'm actually shocked to find a small villa instead of a mansion, so I guess their mom just wanted privacy, but she isn't a fan of a huge house.

Before Asher opens the door, he grabs my hand in his and it makes me realize how sweaty mine is.

"Ah, you made it," a short woman greets us, and it takes me a second to realize that it's actually Asher's mom, because she looks very… simple.

He leans in and hugs his mom before he introduces me. "Hi mom. This is Hayley."

"Hi, it's so nice to meet you Mrs. Dawson," I say and extend a hand, but his mom grabs me in a warm hug.

I can't help but think at the fact that he didn't introduce me as his girlfriend.

"Nonsense, call me Diana." She instructs me and grabs my arm to lead me toward the dining room, leaving Asher protesting behind us.

My nerves have calmed a little, but not entirely, especially since I haven't met Sebastian just yet. "Hayley, this is my oldest, Sebastian." She says as soon as my eyes meet the older man who's standing next to the sofa.

"A pleasure," he says and shakes my hand slightly. His eyes bore into mine in an indescribable way that almost made me bristle, but I push that feeling deep down, trying to ignore it.

Despite the unease, I smile. "It's nice to finally meet you, Sebastian."

"Likewise. Shall we?" he gestures toward the table and places a hand on the small of my back leaving me frozen on the spot.

I use every ounce of strength not to slap his hand away and join Asher at the table where he's chatting with his mom. I take a sit next to him and release a short breath when I see Sebastian taking the seat opposite Asher, and not opposite me.

"So, Hayley, Asher tells me you're a law student. How's that going for you?" Diana opens the conversation while we're being served food by her helpers.

I place my glass of water down before I answer. "It's great but I'm more than ready to finish."

"I take it it's your final year?" she continues and before I get to answer, Asher places his big palm on my thigh almost making me jump but I don't react in any way.

"Yes. Only a few months left before my bar exam." I explain and smile politely.

Diana does the same. "My father, Asher's grandfather was a lawyer. He always hoped I'd follow in his footsteps, but business was more my power."

"Forgive me for asking this, brother, but I can't contain my curiosity. Do you have any sisters, Hayley? You are incredibly beautiful, so I'm hoping there might be more of you," Sebastian intervenes and both Asher and I tense at the same time.

I place my hand on top of Asher's in a quiet request to let me handle him. "No, I'm afraid I don't." It's all I say, without thanking him for his compliment.

I will not entertain this conversation anymore.

"Okay, let's eat before the food gets cold." Diana ends any continuation, and we all dive into our food quietly.

EIGHT | HAYLEY

PRESENT DAY

We enter the bar very soon after we've left the apartment, and because I rent a place very close to Asher's penthouse, I hope I won't see him tonight. I can't deal with him anymore.

I need to drink and forget everything that's happened over the last few days.

"Two vodka martinis, please," Jennifer orders as soon as we take a seat at the bar.

If I'm correct, it's Thursday, so the bar isn't very crowded, which is very pleasing if I'm being honest.

"You know what we should do? We should go to New York for the weekend. We deserve some fun. You remember the last time we were there?" Jen shoots an idea that actually doesn't sound so bad, especially since we just reconnected.

We could use some time together, and I could use some time away from Westport. "You mean the time when I broke up with Asher because of Sebastian?"

Jen cringes. "You always felt something was off about that guy."

"That I did, and I didn't trust my instincts," I say nostalgically, wishing that I could rewrite history and events, but I can't.

What's done, it's done. "I think it's a great idea."

"Great. I'll take care of flights," she announces with an excited smile.

We quickly receive our drinks and raise them to toast. "To us. We made it so far," I say, and we click them together with a cheer.

While I take a sip from my cold and refreshing drink, my eyes land on a man standing at a table behind Jen. When he catches my eye, he smiles proudly and raises his glass in greeting, bringing a smile on my lips. "I think I found my fuck for tonight," I announce proudly, although I'm almost a hundred percent sure that's a lie.

I haven't been able to let another man touch me so far, and trust me, I tried.

I tried therapy, and hypnotherapy and even women. Nothing helps, and although the guy is good-looking, he does nothing for me, really.

"Good for you. Juliana is out of town so no sex for me tonight," she continues and waits for my reaction. When the information reaches my brain, my eyes bulge out of my sockets, and I almost spill my drink.

"You and Juliana got back together?"

Jen bursts out laughing at my reaction. "Yes. We did and we'd been inseparable since then. I'm actually going to propose because she's carrying our baby."

"Oh, my God, Jen, I'm so happy for you." I say proudly and lean in to hug my friend.

My eyes are all teary now, so I grab a napkin from the bar and dab underneath my eyes.

I am truly happy for her. For both of them. This is such beautiful news, and I am proud to call this beautiful and strong woman my friend.

Jen sees me wiping my tears and her smile disappears quickly. "I'm sorry. I... I shouldn't have told you like this."

"What? No. Jen, these are happy tears. Do you know how long it's been since I had happy tears in my eyes? I'm beyond happy for you and I'm even more thrilled to be a part of your happiness again."

Now she's the one wiping at her eyes, so we both burst out laughing. In all honesty though, I couldn't be happier that out of the two of us, at least one made it. My destiny was different, and I will never be jealous of her happiness just because my path took such a horrible turn. "There is something I didn't get to tell you back then or even do something with the information. I think I found my birth mom before everything."

I can tell Jen is shocked by the news. "Really? You never said anything about it back then. Does she live close by?"

"I didn't get a chance. It all happened so fast." I shrug. I want to go on, but I don't get the chance because the guy that's got his eyes on me approaches us with a smirk on his face.

"Hello, ladies. Sorry to interrupt. I was hoping

for a minute alone with this beautiful lady," he says to Jen, so she smiles politely before replying to the comment made by the man. "I need to use the restroom anyways."

I hide my smile in my glass and the gentleman takes Jennifer's seat. "Hi, I'm Dean. I didn't want to interrupt, but I couldn't stay away anymore."

"Is that so?" I chuckle and he gestures the bartender for another two drinks. "Hayley." I say and extend my hand.

His hazel eyes never leave mine as he takes my hand and places a soft kiss on it. The gesture brings back horrible flashbacks, so I find myself jumping out of the seat like it burned me.

He used to look at me like that. From under his eyelashes, like a predator. "Sorry, Dean. I...umm, this isn't a good idea."

"Sorry. Did I do something to upset you?" he asks with genuine concern, so I take a deep breath and sit back down on the high bar stool.

Maybe I should try again. "No... no, Dean. It's the usual, it's not you, it's me." I reply and he laughs at my comment. Okay, maybe I can have a normal conversation with him.

HAYLEY

FOUR YEARS AGO

Last weekend's dinner with Asher's mom and brother felt like the longest thing that I had to sit through in my entire life and when we stepped out the front door, I felt a whoosh of relief.

After we left, we ended up spending another weekend tangled up in each other's arms. And although Asher made sure my thoughts were all about him, I couldn't get Sebastian's following gaze out of my head.

Ash didn't catch on the tension that followed me around for a few days after the dinner and I don't know if I'm okay with that or not.

"Hayley, are you okay?" Asher asks as he hands me a glass off diet coke. It's Thursday night and I was planning to cuddle up in my bed and study while Jen is out, but he surprised me by showing up with Chinese food.

His question doesn't surprise me though. "Yeah. Just tired. It's been a long week."

He seats down next to me on the sofa and faces me. "Then it just proves that my idea is perfect. I was hoping to take you away this weekend."

I knew I'd regret helping Declan. "I wish I could, but I can't. I'm modelling for a friend's photoshoot."

I try to play it cool, but Asher's gaze gets darker by the second. "What kind of photoshoot?"

"He wants to do some boudoir stuff. Something like that," I explain in a dismissive tone. I was hoping he wouldn't mind me doing this but by the reaction he's having, I think he does.

He clears his throat and scoots a little bit closer to me. "I'm going to pretend and hope that you don't know what boudoir means, Hayley."

"I know very well what boudoir means, Ace."

He chuckles and then plasters on a straight face. Is he seriously upset? "You're not doing this!" He says with finality, and I don't know what pisses me off more, his tone or his dated ideas.

I jump off the sofa and turn around to face him. I raise an accusatory finger at his face. "You don't get to tell me what to do, Asher. That's not how a relationship works!"

"It is when it's about you getting naked in front of someone else but e!" He stands up from the sofa and fights back. Arguing with your boyfriend is not the greatest when he's a head taller and you have to look up at him, but he's not winning this argument.

"Asher, it's modelling. I'm not prostituting myself and no one will even see my face. No one will know it's me!" I say with a deep sigh and start massaging my temples with two fingers.

Ash's jaw clenches just before he shouts. "*I* will know that it's you!"

I close my eyes for a second before I blow out another long and shaky breath. "I won't have this conversation, Asher. You can't tell me what I can and can't do! It doesn't work like that!"

"I wouldn't even dream of telling you what to do, but this is different. I could never stand by while another man sees your body." He takes two strides and grabs my waist possessively. "This body belongs to me, and only me, Hayley. It's the only way this relationship will work because otherwise I'll have to poke his eyes out and feed them to my lions."

Lions? He's probably joking.

"Asher..." I drawl and he kisses my jaw, fully knowing that he's won this battle. If I'm putting myself in his position, I'd probably kill a woman that's about to see him half naked too. "Fine. You win."

He smirks and wraps his arms tighter around me. "I thought you knew by now that I am extremely possessive, Hayley, and that this ass," he drawls and grabs my ass in his big palms, "belongs to me."

He starts with slow kisses from my jaw, down on my neck and uses his palms to raise my butt, making me straddle him. When he starts moving, I assume that he's heading for my room, but he's only using the wall to support my body.

I'm wearing a night pyjama dress, and my thin

underwear does nothing to protect me from the growing monster in his sweats and my mind forgets any reason why doing it in my common living room while Jen could walk in on us, isn't a good idea.

Asher holds me tight with his left arm while he uses his right to push his sweats and boxers down his legs and to rip my panties. "You see what you're doing to me, baby? I can bet every man has the same reaction when they would see your beautiful body, and you want me to be okay with it?" he grits out and pushes himself inside me with one swift move.

A loud moan escapes my lips at the harsh intrusion, but it quickly turns into moans of pleasure. "Asher."

"Yes, baby. You like it against the wall?" he whispers in my ear and thrusts deep and steady.

I lean my head on the wall. "Yes. Yes. I think it's my favorite position."

"Yeah? Let's see if I can change your mind, baby," he adds and one second later he walks over to the rug. "Bend over." He orders me and I do it with excitement.

I get down in all fours and he takes me from behind. He intensifies his thrusts and slaps me on my ass cheeks occasionally. "Okay, I stand corrected," I breathe out and use my right hand to rub my clit while he holds my weight with his left hand and supports himself with his right one.

"Yes, Asher. It's so good," I whimper, and his

thrusts hit even deeper if that's possible, knocking the breath out of me.

I open my mouth to speak again when the front door opens widely, and a shocked but amused Jen stands wide eyed in the doorway.

"Oh, shit." I say first and Asher's next to fly off of me and cover himself with the throw that was on the sofa. I'm so sorry," I say as soon as I get up and after she closes the door behind her, Jen bursts out laughing.

"Should I go? I'm gonna go," Ash mutters and grabs his hoodie. I think this is the first time I see Ash embarrassed and I have to admit it's not a reaction I thought I'd see from him, but maybe he was just taken by surprise.

If anything, I think I would've expected him to ask her to join in.

I nod and chuckle. "I'll call you later."

A bit less embarrassed now that he's fully dressed, he places a chaste kiss on my lips and smiles at Jen before he exits our apartment.

"I'm so sorry, it… things escalated quickly," I explain, and Jennifer laughs even harder.

She takes her jacket off and throws herself on the sofa only to jump back on her feet a millisecond later. "You didn't do it on the sofa, did you?"

"No."

She sits back down and gestures for me to sit next to her. I approach slowly and make sure that no private parts are showing now that I don't have any underwear.

"Please don't do it here again, but girl, that dick? Yay you!" she surprises me, and we both burst out laughing again. "You didn't say he was coming tonight; I would've stayed at Declan's."

My smile doesn't change. "I didn't know either. He brought dinner. Shit, I have to tell Declan I can't do the photoshoot anymore."

"Why not?" she asks with a frown.

I chew on the inside of my cheek. "Asher doesn't like the idea of me being naked in front of Dec, and for my body to be displayed in his work."

I can tell she's a bit taken aback by my news by the deep frown on her forehead. "Asher doesn't like it? Since when you care what a man lets you do with *your* body?"

I sigh. "I really like him, Jen."

"I know you do, honey, but isn't that a bit toxic?" she continues with a worried expression on her beautiful features.

It just downs on me how gorgeous my friend is. Her curly sand blonde hair fits her sharp face perfectly and her green eyes can read into your soul.

"Maybe, but you said it yourself, that dick…" I try to play it cool, and she smiles.

"You let me know if it gets too much. If *he* gets too much. Now, you said something about Chinese?" she ends the conversation and looks around for the mentioned food.

NINE | ASHER

PRESENT DAY

Since I came back to Westport my life has been all about the company my damn brother left behind, but for the past week, it feels like it's actually been about Hayley, Sebastian, and their fucking secrets.

Finding myself in dire need of a drink, I decide to leave my penthouse and head to the bar I used to go after Hayley left me.

I reach the bar in under 5 minutes and when I open the door, my heart almost stops beating in my chest. It hasn't beaten properly in a very long time anyway, but now, seeing her chatting happily with that man, I don't know if I want to rip his throat out or throw her on my shoulder and take her back to my apartment.

Or both.

I stroll toward them with a hard face on and when she notices me, she almost jumps out of the chair in surprise, but I don't believe one second that she's actually scared of my reaction, because in all truth, she never got to see me react when I'm furious.

When I found her with my brother in that hotel

room, I was more hurt than furious.

"Mr Dawson, it's nice to meet you. I actually work at the company. Dean Briggs, it's a pleasure." I listen to him out of boredom but when he extends a hand, I merely watch it for a split second then turn my attention to the woman next to him.

She shouldn't be here, but even worse, she shouldn't be talking to another man. I cannot stand seeing her so close to him.

"Hayley, let's go," I say in a demanding tone, forgetting the reason that I came for in the first place, and even more important, forgetting that she's not mine.

"I'm not going anywhere with you, Ace!" she slurs, and I raise a brow in question. She knows I hate it when she calls me Ace.

I have to blow out a deep breath before I grit out. "The hell you aren't. I'll take you home."

I grab her hand to pull her off her chair when the man stops me. He gets up and a bit too in my face for his own good. "Hey man, if she wants to stay, she can stay."

I huff a laugh. "No one asked you."

"Listen, just because you're a millionaire, doesn't mean you should treat people like this," he replies.

"Billionaire," I correct him with a snarl, but don't use my energy to look in his direction. My eyes remain trailed on the woman in front of me.

"Still applies."

"Hayley, you're drunk, and I don't trust this guy to take care of you, so let's go, now," I try again before I lose my temper but when she doesn't move a finger to come with me, I throw her a wicked grin. Then I grab her from the waist, throw her on my shoulder, and carry her out of the bar, ignoring the guy's protests and Jen's wide eyes.

"Put me down, Ace!" she snarls at me, and I chuckle.

I'm sure she was going for scary, but it just came out cute.

"I said I'm taking you home."

But I'm not, really. I'm taking her to the penthouse because it's closer and although she's very thin, I can't carry her for 3 blocks.

"You are such a brute; Jennifer is in there."

"You can text her. She'll survive."

We reach the penthouse very quickly and I head straight for the bedroom and place her gently on my bed. I pull out her phone from her purse and ask for her code. She doesn't answer and somehow, I get the idea of trying the date when we first met at the club and when it works, I gasp in shock.

What's the truth? Was I really the fool Jennifer led me believe that I was?

"Don't leave me, Ace," she whispers with her eyes closed and I'm not sure if I should answer.

I sit down at the edge of the bed and pull the covers on top of her. "I'm not going anywhere, baby," I find myself whispering while I caress her right cheek.

God, how it hurts to see her like this. She's so beautiful, yet so fragile.

"Don't let him have me. I want you. I'll always want you and he knows it, that's why he's so aggressive all the time. You are the reason of my pain. You are the reason he beats me." Her words stop my hand in mid-air, and I think that I forget to breathe for a second.

Deep down I know who she talks about, but I just can't bring myself to accept it. I sit up straight and try to process what she's saying.

It can't be true.

It just can't.

"Who beats you, Hayley?" I ask in another strained whisper.

"He does. Every night. He's a monster. Sebastian's a monster and I'll never escape him. You're never going to save me."

Her words hit me like a sledgehammer, and I stagger back a few steps. I quickly realize that I've stopped breathing and I gasp for air. Somehow tears roll down my cheeks, but I don't feel anything.

I just feel empty.

Deep and hollow emptiness.

I was wrong…

I was so fucking wrong.

ASHER

FOUR YEARS AGO

"I have good news, Asher. Everything is ready for your move to London, little brother," Sebastian announces as soon as he walks inside my office as if it's something worthy of celebration when it's most definitely not. I completely forgot about the plan for my move to London.

I laugh bitterly and stand. "You'll have to find someone else for the London office, brother. I'm not going for now. You'll have to share this with me for a little while longer."

Sebastian's smile falters, but he doesn't say anything for a while.

I head toward the big window and take in the beautiful view of the city.

Westport is not huge, but it's big enough for us to have the most successful marketing company in the state, and now with a branch in London.

The plan was for me to run that one, but until Hayley finished her degree, I won't be able to go anywhere.

"Asher, we had an agreement," he suddenly grits out and I find myself turning around and narrowing my eyes at him.

"It looks like you're confusing me with an employee, brother." I growl and head back toward my office chair with steady steps.

Sebastian is very good at confrontation, whereas I try to avoid it when possible, but he knows that when I'm furious, someone might lose their head. "That wasn't my intention, Asher, but we had clear plans. Important ones, and now you're telling me that all that's changed because of a woman?"

"Leave Hayley out of this!"

Sebastian blows out an annoyed breath. "How can I do that when she's the reason you've changed your mind?"

"This conversation should've been over 2 minutes ago. I'm not going there, so get used to the idea, Sebastian!" I say with finality and before my brother gets another reply, Hayley walks in with a smile on her face.

A smile that dies the moment she sees my brother, who also scoffs at the sight of my girlfriend. "Ah, the woman of the hour."

Hayley frowns, clearly confused by my brother's words. "Oh, did I interrupt something?"

"Not really. It's safe to say it involves you," he continues his attack, so I decide to step in.

"Sebastian, back off," I warn my brother and walk over to greet my girl with a kiss. I am actually beyond happy to see her.

Sebastian rolls his eyes at us like a diva and heads for the door. "Fine. This conversation isn't over, Ash."

Hayley remains frowning as I invite her to take a seat on the sofa. "What's that all about?"

"My brother is pushing this idea for me to move to London and run our office there, but now is under the impression that I'm not going because I met you." When Hayley's frown deepens, I curse myself for not finding a different side to the story.

Now she's going to believe she's to blame, and who knows, maybe ask me to go.

"Can I be honest with you, Ash?" She asks and I nod, nudging her to go on. "I... Ever since the dinner I have this feeling about your brother that I can't shake, and you know... I'm wondering if the feeling could be mutual. Maybe he doesn't like me."

"You don't like Sebastian?"

I had a hint that something wasn't good between them, but I can't really say why they dislike each other.

"It's not that I don't like him... he just, he's intense, alright?" she says with a deep sigh and averts her gaze with embarrassment.

"Regardless, I'm not going. I was never a fan of the idea and now I have an extra reason to stay, and he has to deal with it."

Hayley leans toward the small coffee table and pours herself a glass of water. My throat is also dry, but I need something a lot stronger right now, but it's barely after midday.

I stand up from the armchair and sit next to her on the sofa. "Hey, don't be upset. I'll deal with it.

Sebastian is all bark but no bite. You don't have to worry about him. He'll come around."

"Okay," she whispers. "I came to grab lunch with you by the way."

"Ok, that sounds great."

"I'll just run to the restroom really quick and then we can go."

TEN | HAYLEY

PRESENT DAY

I open my eyes slowly and I quickly realize that I am the proud owner of a giant migraine, so I wince in pain. It's what I get for wishing a cure for heartbreak and madness. I place my head in my hands for a few long seconds to calm the throbbing pain in the front of my skull.

A second later I realize that I can't remember how I got home, so I raise my head from my palms and look around me and shock rolls through me like a bucket of ice water.

I'm in Asher's bedroom.

I jump out of the bed like it's on fire and start pacing around the room. How did I even get here? What happened last night?

I should go, but what if he's waiting for me? How will I deal with that?

Hoping that he's not home anymore, I open the door and enter the living room. I quickly find Asher standing with a concerned look on his face and I know that I'm not getting away that easily.

I take a deep breath in before he opens his mouth. "Was he beating you, Hayley?"

Does his question shock me? A little.

Does it scare me? Not at all.

But it does open me up to feeling all that pain I've been immune to for a very long time.

Whatever happened last night that I don't remember of, does not sound good.

"What?" I choke out a single word.

"Last night you spoke in your sleep, so there's no going back now, Hayley. You're going to answer my questions. Was my brother abusive to you?" He asks again and this time takes a few steps to close the distance between us and I feel cornered.

"He was so much more than abusive. He was a monster," I let the words escape past my lips and I feel all the walls I had brought up inside, crumble down like paper.

And when he falls on his knees the room starts spinning around me and tears start falling like a faucet. It's not an image I ever dreamed of seeing again. "No more lies, Hayley. Please. Please tell me everything, baby."

A wave of emotions rolls through me, and I find myself falling on my knees right in front of him. Seeing him so emotional, raw, and scared, it does something inside of me that I can't even explain it.

Until now hate kept me fuelled for what I had planned to do. It was easy, but if hate no longer exists between us, I can't keep it all locked up inside anymore. So, I take his beautiful face in my palms and tell him everything.

While we sob in between words, I tell him about the night at the hotel and everything that followed afterward. I tell him about how he cut me off from my friends, and my college and how he sexually abused me every time he found me crying because he knew that was when I was so broken that I'd beg him to stop, and that was his favorite part.

"The night he died, he beat me up so badly that no makeup could cover me up, so he had to leave without me," I tell him with a broken smile when I remember that night.

Asher's shoulders shake while he sobs loudly. "I'm so sorry. I'm so sorry, Hayley. Forgive me, forgive me, baby. Please forgive my damned soul for being so stupid. So blind and ignorant. Forgive me because I'll never be able to forgive myself for what my brother has done to you."

Then I tell him Sebastian's reason. "He's your half-brother, Asher. Your mother raised him because your father took him away from his own when she got depressed, but you're half-brothers and he hated having to share the company with you."

"I can't believe I've been lied to my entire life and then my brother... he wrecked your life without as much as a second thought. God, how I wish he was alive just so I could kill him myself," he says through gritted teeth and wipes his face with the back of his hand. He takes my face in his palms now and sticks his forehead to mine and I shudder.

I missed him so fucking much that having him so close now, makes me want to curl up and cry for hours because I never thought this would ever happen again.

"Everything I endured... I was so scared. So, so scared that he would do something to you, or you to him if you found out. So, I kept quiet. I kept quiet while he took me until I was raw. I kept quiet while he pounded his fists at me with no remorse. I kept quiet for 3 years, thinking that it would be an eternity. But it wasn't. I made it out. Albeit with a shattered soul and a broken spirit, I made it out."

I take a deep breath before I continue. "I shouldn't have come back or stayed in this town, but when I saw you that day, the hate in your eyes, it felt like even beyond his grave, he won. So, I had to do this for me. After 3 awful long years, I got to do something for myself, and I chose this. I chose revenge, to bury his company because although he was obsessed with me soon after he met me, this company was his greatest love."

Asher's eyes are full of understanding and rage, both in equal amounts and it's a devastating look on him, but I can't let myself love him again, because I'm afraid it'll never be the same.

I will never be the same.

"I have missed you so much," I whisper and caress the side of his face. "But I have to do this," I add, and another tear burns the side of my cheek.

Asher nods slowly in understanding.

"I know, baby. I know."

He kisses the tips of my fingers, a gesture that used to thrill me in the past and make butterflies swirl in my stomach. Now it has a heart-clenching effect because I know nothing will ever be like in the past. "Let's do it together," he adds with seriousness and shock rolls through me once more.

I stare into the grey ooze of Asher's eyes for a long minute, trying to figure out if he's toying with me.

Can I actually trust him after everything? Can I ever trust another man after everything?

HAYLEY

FOUR YEARS AGO

The restaurant we had lunch at is right across Asher's office building because he swears their food is healthy and good and it's not like I know a better place.

Before we finish our lunch and part ways, I head toward the restroom to wash my hands. I watch myself in the mirror while I do it and can't ignore how ever since I last saw Sebastian at the office, I have the same uneasy feeling in the pit of my stomach.

A second later, the door opens behind me, and my heart skips a beat at the sight of the dark-haired man approaching the sink next to mine while his eyes don't leave mine in the mirror.

He can probably read the shock on my face, because he feels the need to clarify. "Unisex bathroom."

"Oh."

When he's done washing, he grabs a few paper towels and uses them to dry his hands. It's funny how it just downs on me that his built is a bit smaller than Ash's, yet somehow, he looks scarier.

"Do you have a problem with me, Hayley?"

I do have a problem with him. God is my witness when I say that something is fucking off about this man, but I can't just blatantly tell him that, so I turn his own question against him. "Do you?"

"I have a problem with my brother being stupid darling, not with you per se."

I snort. "I think it's obvious that I'm the reason he is not moving to London, so it's safe to assume that you're not my biggest fan because of that."

Sebastian smiles and takes a step closer to me, which isn't really great for my fast-beating heart. "Smart and beautiful. What's there not to like?"

His comment makes me cringe once again and I have to fight hard not to bristle. "I really like your brother, Sebastian."

He takes two further steps and I hold my breath until he speaks again. "And I really like you," he whispers so close that I can actually feel his breath on my face, but what he does next blows my mind and leaves me stunned for several long seconds.

Sebastian smashes his lips onto mine so brutally and forcefully that I am too shocked to react in any way for a long minute.

Being kissed by Sebastian Dawson is the last thing I was expecting him to do, so it takes me a long time to realize what's happening and to smash both my palms onto his chest and to push him away with all my strength.

"What the fuck?" I spit and take a few more steps backwards to make sure that there's enough space between us so he won't try this again.

I wipe my mouth angrily and before I can stop, I slap him harshly across the face. "I am with your brother! Why would you do that?"

"I don't fucking know! Trust me, I wish I did." He replies and I don't know what's more bizarre and disturbing, him kissing me or him saying that he doesn't know why he did it.

"You dare to fucking touch me again and I'll break your hands!"

He smirks, completely throwing me off. "Hmm, feisty, just how I like them."

"Stop this, Sebastian. I wouldn't want to ruin your relationship with your brother for a mistake," I say through gritter teeth and grab the door handle, ready to leave when his next words ring behind me.

"Good, because I wouldn't want to ruin your life."

I turn around like a storm and push at his chest again. "Is that a threat?"

"No, just an observation."

I huff a laugh, roll my eyes at him and exit the bathroom before this gets worse or before Asher comes looking for me.

When I return to our table, I find him chatting to a girl, roughly the same age as me and I have to admit, seeing the way she plays with her arm brings out a feral growl out of me, which I have to push back down before I make next to my boyfriend.

How do I interrupt their conversation and let her know he's mine in the same sentence? "I'm ready to go, babe." I pretend to not have seen her for a second. "Oh, hello. I'M Hayley."

The brunette scoots a few inches away from my man but doesn't deign to return the introduction or shake my extended hand.

Bitch.

"Freya, this is my girlfriend, Hayley. Babe, this is an old friend, Freya." Ash stands up and grabs me by the waist, bringing a huge smile on my face.

I think we're both aware of my jealousy fit, but I don't care.

Freya joins us and stands up facing us. "Oh. Right. I didn't know you got tied down. I thought you said you don't want a girlfriend when we hooked up."

Wow.

Asher chuckles softly, but I can tell he's pissed by Freya's lack of class. "I think it's time for you to go, Freya."

"This was a complete waste of time anyway," she scoffs and grabs her purse in a rush. On the way out, she brushes my shoulder and exits with a grimace on her face.

Ash turns to face me with narrowed eyes. "*Babe?*"

I avert my gaze. "She was touching your arm." I whisper and continue to look a different way until he grabs my chin between his two fingers and forces me to look him in the eyes.

"Don't be embarrassed. You're adorable when you're jealous. You should've seen your face." He kisses my temple and then my lips.

"I hope I'll still be adorable when I tell you that I'm going away for the weekend with Jennifer." I say with a childish smile and a half-closed eye.

Asher seems to be thinking for a minute, so I urge him to start moving because we're still standing in the middle of the restaurant. "What if I come with you?"

"No way. It's a girl's trip, Ace. You can't." I protest with a laugh. I know he doesn't really want to come with us.

When we make it in front of the tower, we both stop, and he wraps his arms around me. "Okay. Fine... but know that I was planning to keep you hot and naked all weekend."

"Dang it. I'm bummed that I'll miss it." I laugh and he gives me another kiss before I say my goodbyes and head for the bus stop with a smile on my face.

ELEVEN | ASHER

PRESENT DAY

"I wrote you a letter," she whispers and wipes her tears away.

God, she's so pretty that I'm in actual pain having to watch her cry. I've always only given her tears and hurt.

Everything she went through, was because of me and I was so fucking blind. "I never received anything." I whisper and stroke her hair softly.

"Of course you didn't because he found it before I got to mail it," she says with a raise of her right shoulder. There's so much this tiny woman had to endure and the fact that she's standing here in front of me today is an absolute miracle.

Even worse than that? It was all because of me.

"Can you tell me about it?" I ask with my eyes closed. If she could survive that, I have to hear it for her.

"He made me read it out to him while he fucked me like an animal, over and over again for several hours," she says and shudders at the memory.

Her back is to the sofa, so she rests her head on the soft cushion.

There's so much distance between us that I wish I could reach for her hand again, but I don't. I feel that she might be too vulnerable for me to touch her right now.

Rage drives me to my feet, and I need to let it out before I explode from it, so I grab a chair and throw it around to room, but quickly come to realize that this will just traumatize her even more when she covers her ears with her palms, so I run toward her and grab both her hands in mine. "No, no, no. I'm so sorry. I shouldn't have done that. I'm sorry, baby."

She nods and bites her bottom lip.

"What can I do to... fuuck! I don't even know what to say. I know I can't fix it. I can't erase it, so how can I help?" I ask and her eyes never leave mine, not even for a second.

"There's nothing you can do to make it all go away. On top of everything your brother did to me, you hurt me too, Asher. I can't forget how up until yesterday you hated me and didn't want me here." Her next words come as a punch in my gut, and I fight the urge to stumble back.

"Hayley, I never hated you. I never stopped loving you. You have to believe me," I manage to choke out but even I don't sound convinced, how could I ever convince her?

Her smile is sad, and she shakes her head slowly. Does she not believe me?

Who am I kidding?

Of course, she doesn't. I put her through hell.

Both me and my brother and what's worse, everything she had to endure was because of me. Because she met me.

"If that's what your love looks like now, Asher, then I don't want it," she sighs and looks away from me, unable to meet my gaze. "He hurt me. He hurt me physically, but I still hoped that somewhere far away, you still loved and still cared for me, so I could get through everything if I had that. But when you came back for his funeral... and now, the hate, and rage in your eyes, took that hope away from me."

Hayley is crying and her voice breaks every two words, and I don't even realize that I've been crying too until she reaches to wipe away my tears.

"I'm so sorry, baby. I'm sorry that in a way I've helped to your breaking. Please find it in you to forgive me for being so, so stupid and ignorant. I'll be waiting, no matter how long. Hayley, baby, I'll be waiting forever if I have to because you deserve that. You deserve the world and if you do decide that you can't forgive me, I'll respect that. Because I do love you. For a long time, I think I confused hurt and hate, because Hayley, I was hurting, not hating you. I could never hate you when I was madly in love with you."

Every word I say is honest and truthful. I will do anything in my power to get her back, keep her safe, and love her, but at the same time, I will back out if that's what she needs me to do.

"I love you too, Asher, but I need time. I have

to believe that we could get back together before I let it happen," she says, and I realize that I held my breath the entire time and now I'm breathing normally again.

Sebastian Dawson, I hope you rot in hell for the life you destroyed.

"Of course, baby. I'm never letting you go again. Never, Hayley. I swear on my worthless life."

She's been in a literal hellhole for the past 3 years and she's worried about hurting me. The things she had to go through, just to protect me, a guy he knew for 2 weeks, is unbearable for weak souls and somehow, I remember when I told her she's become a shell of a woman my heart breaks all over again.

She didn't deserve any of the shit I've put her through on top of everything Sebastian has done to her. So I have no idea how I'll ever be able to repay her sacrifice.

How the fuck can I ever let her go again? I'll go to fucking hell and back before I leave her alone again and that's not a promise.

It's an oath.

ASHER

FOUR YEARS AGO

It's dinner time with Sebastian and Mom again, but this time Hayley decided to skip it and honestly, I was totally fine with it.

I meant what I said before she met them the first time that if they don't like her, then I'll be okay with it, and now I'm even more sure of it.

Because I think I'm falling in love with this woman.

"So, how's things with Hayley?" Mom asks between bites and Sebastian's ears perk up.

I throw a short look toward my brother, then turn my attention back to mom. "Better than ever. She's away this weekend and I already miss her."

"See, he's being pussy whipped!" Sebastian protests and raises an accusatory fork at me.

Mom rolls her eyes. "Language, Sebastian!"

"It's the truth."

I wipe my mouth and set my napkin down. "You're fucking nuts, can't you see it? What do you have against Hayley?" I ask calmly and turn my attention on him.

Sebastian snickers like a teenager and looks me

dead in the eye. "She kissed me, that's what I have against her. When you were having lunch today, I ran into her in the restroom, and she kissed me."

I don't know if I'm shocked, furious or hurt. "I'm done here." I say with composed calm and throw my napkin on my plate before I jump onto my feet and head for the door, ignoring my mom's protests.

There's only one person who can calm me right now, so I head for Hayley's apartment.

***

An hour later I knock on her door and Jen is the one to open the door for me. "Is Hayley here?"

"She's in her bedroom. Asher, whatever this is, it isn't a good idea. She had a very crappy day," her friend stops me before I step in.

I blow out a deep breath and nod with understanding. I'll try to not get too worked up about what my brother said, although my blood is boiling right now.

Jen steps aside and I head toward Hayley's bedroom. When I push the door open, I find her curled up in bed with tears in her eyes, and for a split second I forget why I came here in the first place. "Baby, what's wrong?"

When she raises her teary gaze at me, her face changes and she quickly wipes at her eyes. It doesn't help though because they're red and puffy, a sign that she's been crying for hours.

She clears her throat as I sit on the bed and soften my gaze. "Nothing. Allergies."

"Please don't lie to me," I whisper and brush my thumb underneath her eyes.

Hayley takes a deep breath and begins fidgeting. "I started looking for my birth mom a while ago, and I found her, so today I decided to go ask about her. She... she has another daughter. I have a sister, and she never looked for me." Once again, she breaks down in sobs so I leave my questions aside and scoot closer so I can wrap her in my embrace.

"Did you meet her... talk to her?"

She shakes her head. "No. I rang the bell and their maid opened. She was at work. They have a huge house, Asher. They have..."

"Shh. It's okay. You don't need any of that. You made it this far on your own, and from now on, I'll bring you the world, Hayley, if that's what will bring your smile back."

She manages a tiny smile and I continue to stroke her hair. "I love you, Hayley. I know it's early and you're going to think that I'm crazy, but I love you too much to see you hurt."

Hayley scoots more toward the headboard of her bed as if she's trying to get away from me. "What do you mean?"

"I mean that meeting her could lead to possible answers for questions you never thought to ask, that's all." I say what's been crossing my mind ever since she spoke about her mother.

Hayley takes a deep breath in. "I know... I do, but

still… I want to know where I come from. What if I have siblings or what if I'm not alone in this world?"

I nod. She isn't wrong. If I were in her place, I'd probably want to know too.

"It's not a mother that I'm looking for, Asher. It's family, a sister, a brother maybe." She adds with a sad smile that breaks my heart into a million pieces.

What I say next comes out faster than I get time to actually filter what I'm saying, but I still don't regret it. "I'll be your family. Hell, I'll give you one right now, just say the word baby."

She chuckles. "Ash, we just met a few weeks ago. We haven't even said…"

"I love you." I fill in for her and it wasn't even a question. "I'm serious, Hayley. I love you."

I grab her hands, but I can still see in her eyes that she doesn't believe me fully. "You can't be serious."

"I don't need more months to know that I love you. Baby, I fell for you the minute I laid eyes on you, and you're telling me I can't love you? I do, I love you and there's nothing that could change how I feel." I say with pure honesty and capture her lips in a passionate kiss but then while she smiles on my lips, I remember what Sebastian said and I pull away.

"What's wrong?" she's quick to ask, aware of the change in my posture. I ponder over if I should tell her what Sebastian said or not.

"Nothing," I reply and throw her a tiny smile in hopes that she'll let it go.

"Oh, my God. Why are you here anyway? Wasn't tonight your family dinner? Din Jennifer call you?" She's now fully shocked and worried.

I sigh and avert my gaze. "Dinner was cut short."

"Why?" She asks and wipes her wet cheeks again.

I take a deep breath while I try to formulate my question. "Sebastian said something that made me lose my appetite. He said you kissed him at the restaurant."

I'm very much aware that there might've been more diplomatic ways to ask her if it's true, but still, I tried not to sound too accusatory. She's shocked and somewhat hurt. I can see it in her eyes, but let's make one thing clear anyway, I don't believe Sebastian's words, however, I know deep down that there's something going on with them.

The thing she does next shock and thrill me at the same time. She jumps off the bed like a tornado and heads for the door with a furious curse. "I'm going to fucking kill him!"

Honestly, I have no idea how I reacted so quickly, but it only takes me a second before I wrap both my arms around her waist and pull her away from the door. "Ash, baby, please tell me you see what he's trying to do." She pleads with me.

"I do. I know, baby. I didn't believe him. It just... messed with me a bit. I'm sorry, he always does that." I explain but don't release her from my grip.

"I love you, Asher. I love you, too, and thinking for a brief second that you believed your brother, terrified me to my very soul." She's holding my face in both her palms and when her lips settle on top of mine, my mind goes blank.

I already told her that I loved her a few minutes before and hearing it back so soon is just everything I could've ever dreamed of.

And Sebastian will pay for his lies.

I'll make sure of that.

TWELVE | HAYLEY

PRESENT DAY

"I should go home now, Jennifer is waiting for me there," I say and start putting my shoes on without looking at Asher at all. For some reason, this is heavier than it should feel, but I just can't shake the feeling that we're not friends and we'll never be.

"I'm happy you two are friends again," he replies with an honest smile, so I try to return one of my own but I'm not too sure it came out right.

"Yeah, it's been nice to have her in my life again, even if it's only been a few days. I'm truly grateful."

Asher wraps his arms around me before I can protest, but I actually let the embrace settle in. This feels right. Perfect, even. "Will I see you later? Let me take you to dinner tonight." He says after he took a step back but still holding my hands in his.

"Of course. We can do that," it's all I say with a genuine smile, and he kisses my cheek cheerfully. The usual swarm of butterflies start swirling low in my belly, giving me a feeling that I thought I'd lost forever.

"I'll walk you downstairs." He suggests and we both make our way to the elevator and after the door close, silence settles between us like fog, almost making it unbearable to breathe.

Thankfully, we reach the ground floor quickly and we exit the elevator into the lobby, where I start walking like my life depends on it.

"Hey, slow down, are you that eager to get away from me?" He says with a chuckle.

"No, I'm eager to get away from their view," I grit out and when the realization hits Asher, he swears under his breath.

"I didn't realize it, I'm sorry," he says when we reach the sidewalk. "No taxi today, you're taking my car," he adds and leads me toward his 8-seat comforter. I don't fight him because I'm just too exhausted. I just smile, shake my head, and climb onto the back seat where we hold so many memories of our first weeks together.

Eddie drives off soon after Asher says something to him, and my eyes remain trained on the man standing on the sidewalk as the car starts moving away.

My stomach is in knots and my heart beats fast in my chest. I don't even know how to describe what's happening right now. How I'm feeling, or why I'm feeling all of the things that I'm feeling.

"You need to focus, Hayley," I whisper to myself and sink in the huge chair. Before I have time to actually process what happened last night, we make it to Jennifer's apartment, which is the apartment we shared in College, so I thank Eddie and exit the car.

It only takes her a knock to open the door and greet me with arms wide open. "You look exhausted. What happened last night?"

I close the door behind me, and we both sit on the sofa. "I told him everything."

It's safe to say that Jennifer is shocked, because her eyes double in size and she places the palm of her right hand over her open mouth. "You did?"

"Mhm." I nod. "I had to. I spoke in my sleep, so I couldn't lie to him anymore."

"He took you to his penthouse? I thought he's just going to take you back to your apartment." She says with a bit too much excitement.

I throw her a look that she understands all too well. "I don't know what to do."

"Did you know what to do before last night?" she asks with a frown, which makes me think long and hard. Did I?

I chew on my bottom lip. "I thought I did. I still think I do… but I'm not too sure how him knowing the truth will affect my plans."

"Can I ask what those plans are?"

I smile. "Diplomatic as always. I want to make sure that men like Sebastian are put away and women in my situation are helped properly. I'm opening a foundation for abused women with the money from my part of the company. I'm going to sell it and I know that any chance that I could have at getting back with Ash will vanish as soon as he finds out."

"You can't know that. If you went down the

path of telling him the truth, you have to tell him everything, and give him some credit," she tells me her opinion and I release a deep sigh.

I know she's right, but I don't know if I'm ready for Asher's reaction. "We're having dinner tonight."

"That's wonderful, Hayley. I'm so happy for you."

I huff a laugh. "Don't be. Not until everything's settled, and on the other side, who's to say that after so many years there's still love between us."

She smiles softly. "There is. I 've seen how you look at each other even before he knew."

I reply with a tiny smile and my heart flutters to life when I think about the possibility of getting back together.

***

I tried with every ounce of my strength to keep my composure and wait for the dinner we planned on having later tonight, but I couldn't, so here I am, in his elevator, waiting for it to take me to Asher's penthouse.

When the doors open a few seconds later, I step inside with shaky legs, hoping to find him alone.

I don't.

Not only is he not alone, he's in the company of the woman he's been screwing in front of me a bit over a week ago. "Oh," I manage to utter and stop in my tracks.

They both turn to face me, and I can see the surprise written all over Asher's face.

I harden my jaw and lift my chin up, as if her presence doesn't affect me at all. "I apologise. I didn't think you'd have company." I say with bitterness in my tone and don't miss Asher's shaky breath. He then proceeds to take a step toward me and away from Mickayla.

"She was just leaving after dropping off some folders," he explains and throws a pointed look toward his employee, who is now left open mouthed and offended by his dismissal. "I'll see you at the office," Asher adds a minute later when he understands that his assistant isn't going to move a muscle.

"Boss?" is the only word that leaves her trembling lips.

Asher growls and I flinch. "Do you prefer a good dick or a good paying job?"

I chuckle and huff a laugh at the same time, while Mick hurries away. When the elevator's doors close, I roll my eyes at him. "Good dick?"

I have no clue where this newfound humour is coming from, but I could get used to it because his cheeky smile makes my heart flutter in my chest. "You forgot how I mage you feel, Miss Marshall? I can very quickly remind you." He says with a pointed look and with two long steps, his hard erection is pressed against my crotch.

"Asher," I whisper and take a step back, knowing that my self-control is already very thin and how only a shred is keeping me from tearing into him, when I couldn't let another man touch me for a year since his brother's passing.

"Did you dream about me, Hayley?" he whispers almost inaudible, but I feel it with every fibre of my being and my response is a short nod.

He comes back close to me but before he can touch me, I place the palm of my hand onto his chest. "We need to talk, Asher. There are things you still don't know, and I can't sleep until you do. I'm not stopping. Just because you know the truth, I can't stop what I'm set to do, and that's bringing the Dawson legacy down."

He remains silent for a long moment. "Do you remember what my dream job was when we met 4 years ago?"

I frown. I really don't.

"I wanted to be a firefighter so bad, but my father never allowed it. Then he passed and left me half the company, so I had to stick with the promise I had made. I promised my father on his death bed that I will never let the Dawson name fall into nothingness, but now I want nothing more. You want to see it crumble? I'll make it crumble. I'll burn it to the fucking ground for you, baby."

My mouth drops open and tears start welling in my eyes, but when he finally touches me, I sink into his arms. He grabs my face with both his palms and smashes his sweet lips onto mine with hunger. I gasp and whimper at the first stroke of his tongue around mine as his hand grips my waist tighter.

That's all I ever needed from him to lose my mind. One touch. *One kiss.*

HAYLEY

FOUR YEARS AGO

I gently push Asher onto my bed while my eyes remain trained on his darkening gaze. I lick my lips lustfully and drop on my knees slowly. He watches me like a hawk with dark and danger promising eyes.

"What are you doing?" he whispers and grabs my shaky hands when I reach for his belt.

"I'm going to show you just how much I love you," I say back and after he swallows a lump, he lets go of my hands and clenches his teeth with excitement.

I can see his jaw flexing while I undo his belt and pull his trousers down his legs, revealing the massive dick that's contained beneath his boxer briefs. "You don't have to do this just to prove something."

I chuckle. "You think I want to prove something? Baby, I'm dying to taste you and have you reach so deep down my throat that I'm gonna choke on it. Don't you dare hold back on me, Dawson!"

Asher gasps and as soon as I grab his dick to spring it free of the boxers, he grabs the back of my head and guides me toward his swollen shaft. I open my mouth wide and take him slow and deep. I suck him while he thrusts his hips hard until I can feel his cum on the tip of my tongue and I stop.

I lift the hem of my oversized T-shirt and quickly sit on his lap, taking every inch of him with a moan.

"Fuck, baby. You feel unreal around me," he grunts and grabs my waist with one hand to help me up and back onto his size.

I feel the sweat running down my spine and my nerves are on fire with each deep thrust. "You fuck me so good. I never want to forget how you feel inside of me."

"I'm gonna come. I'm gonna come so deep and good, baby," he growls and bites into my shoulder while his words ignite my body like a comet, and I come all over his dick.

He does the same a second later and grabs my entire body into his arms as if trying to merge our bodies together.

Tonight was hard, fast and quiet because Jen is next door, but I love that he can be both gentle and loving and fast and passionate.

I let my head fall onto his shoulder and close my eyes for a second. I don't want to move. I don't want him to go.

It all just feels perfect.

"Are you going to fall asleep on my dick?" He chuckles and I huff a laugh before I reply. "No. I'm just spent." I get up from his lap and pull the T-shirt over my head and use it to wipe the leaking cum between my legs. Then I grab another one from my dresser and return onto his now fully dressed lap. "I love how a simple visit can turn into a good fuck with you." I add with a satisfied grin, and he kissed my chin.

"A good fuck? Baby, when are you going to admit that it's the best fuck you've ever had in your life?" he tries, and I grin arrogantly.

We both know I never had better and never want to anyway, but I love to see him all worked up. "You still have work to do to prove yourself, Dawson."

I probably shouldn't have said that because a second later I'm sprawled on my back and he's between my legs again.

I giggle like a schoolgirl and let him fuck me into oblivion again.

***

Taking a sudden road trip to New York is not something I hoped to do this weekend when I feel like shit, but when the school dean asks you to go and present the college to a couple of prospect students across different high schools, you comply and do it.

We're walking down 5th Avenue, toward the second high school when from the corner of my eye I catch a glimpse of a man staring at us intently and I stop in my tracks, making Jen bump into me because she wasn't paying attention. "What's wrong?"

"I think that guy's taking pictures of us." I explain and point toward the guy on my right with a huge camera in his hand.

She frowns but doesn't agree nor disagree with me, so I start running toward the man before he gets to run away and hide. "Hey! Were you following us just now?"

He doesn't mind me and turns around to leave when I grab the camera off his hands and start searching through the photos he took, all with me.

Not Jen.

Just me. "What's this?" I ask and when he stretches a hand to grab the camera back from me, I take two steps back.

"Was he following us?" Jen asks as soon as she's standing next to me.

I clench my jaw. "Me. Just me. There are dozens of pictures of me. Who sent you?"

"No one. I liked your features. Give it back." I huff a laugh and slap his hand away.

"Bullshit. Listen buddy, I'm on my period and I'm already pissed off today, so you don't want to mess with me. I know this camera is worth a few thousands, so if you don't want me to smash it, you'll tell me who paid you to follow me."

Jen crosses her arms over her chest and stares the guy down. "We're also lawyers and I'll find a way to make you pay if you don't talk."

"Fine. Fine. It's Asher. Asher Dawson? He asked me to follow you around for a couple of days. He's testing your loyalty or something." He confesses and I don't know if I'm shocked or furious.

Asher did this?

"Thanks." It's all I say and after I throw the camera into his arms, I turn around and hail a cab.

Westport is 30 minutes away from New York, and the fare will be crazy, but I can't let this slide. He had me followed?

He went too far.

"Hayley, where are you going?" Jen shouts behind me.

"To speak with Mr Dawson. You finish here, I have to go." I say as I jump into the cab and ask him to take me directly to the Dawson Tower in Westport.

The entire way home I'm filled with anger and hurt and a feeling deep down that I can't even begin to explain. Something feels off and wrong. Something almost feels evil, and I can't stop shaking.

How could he do this to me? How could he not trust me?

Is this because he believed his brother and he needs proof that I kissed him?

Is this because he's just so possessive and needs to know where I am every second of the day?

When the cab stops and brings me out of my thoughts, I exit like a storm and head for his office. The elevator ride is fast, but it still feels like an eternity before I reach their floor and head toward his office.

On my way to him I pass by Sebastian's office

and when our eyes lock through the window wall, a shudder runs through me turning my blood ice cold and leaving me with a horrible feeling.

I ignore everything anyway and storm into Asher's office like a thunder. "How dare you?" I shout as I walk inside and closer to his desk.

I can see that he's confused by my outburst, but that's probably because he doesn't expect for me to know about his little plan. "Hayley, what's wrong?"

"What's wrong? I'll tell you what's wrong!" I shout and shove at his chest. "You had someone fucking following me and taking pictures of me!"

I am absolutely fucking furious with him and even his frown isn't able to calm me down. "What?"

"In New York. You had someone following me. Why? Are you really that jealous and possessive?" I say through gritted teeth, and I want to claw at his face for how good he is at pretending not to know anything about it.

He opens his mouth and closes it a few times before he actually utters a word. "Hayley, I have no idea what you're talking about."

I blow a deep breath and close my eyes briefly. "I can't do this right now, Ace. I think I need a break."

"I'll take you home," he replies, ready to push everything under the rug, as if nothing's happened.

I take a step away from his extended hand. "I need a break from us, Asher."

He releases an incredulous laugh. "Hayley, don't

joke about this. I promise you that I have no idea what you're talking about."

"If it wasn't you who paid the guy to take pictures of me, then why would he say you did? Why would he name you?" I ask with a frown and before the pieces fall into place for me, they do for him and his face changes.

He blows out a deep breath. "Sebastian. He's trying to break us up. The lie about the kiss, now this…"

Oh, God. He's right.

He truly is a psychopath.

"What are we going to do?" I breathe out in shock.

"We're going to show him that nothing will break us up. We'll make it all public at the company event next Saturday." He explains and I remain silent.

Do I want this? Do I want to become a public figure like he is? If it means that Sebastian will back off, then yes. "Okay."

"Okay."

"I'm so sorry for my reaction. God, how could I be this stupid?" I almost break down in tears, but Asher is quick to wrap his arms around me and to hold me close.

He kisses the top of my head. "Don't apologise, baby. You did nothing wrong, and my brother will pay for this, I promise."

THIRTEEN | HAYLEY

PRESENT DAY

"There's that perfect o shape again," he almost moans. "Baby if you don't close your mouth, I might not be able to stop what's going to happen to you next." He adds with a groan, and I melt in his arms once again.

We are now back at the penthouse and have laid some blankets and pillows on the floor and now sit in front of the fireplace tangled with each other.

"And what would that be, Asher?" I say playfully and bite my lower lip while he watches me with lustful eyes although he had me more than 3 times already.

"It may include those beautiful lips of yours wrapped around my cock, do you want that, baby?" He whispers softly and kisses my neck slowly.

Do I want that?

I want anything this man has to offer me, so I smile sheepishly and start lowering my head while trailing wet kisses on his abdomen. I can feel his breathing slowing with anticipation and I feel a sense of confidence that makes my body heat up.

When I reach the sensitive area around his shaft,

I start kissing around it to build up the tension. I then take it in my hand and Asher gasps so loudly that he startles me. I give it two slow rubs before I lower my mouth to it and wrap my lips around his pink head. When I start swirling my tongue around it, Asher pushes his hips forward to thrust deeper. "God, that's unbelievable."

I smile at his comment and take him deep down my throat making him curse under his breath. In the next second, he jumps to his feet, brings me up on my knees, and grabs the back of my head to help himself fuck my mouth harder and deeper. With each thrust, I can feel his legs shaking. "I'm gonna come, baby. I'm gonna come so fucking good," he breathes, and it only takes him a few more seconds before he shoots hot and salty liquid down my throat. I swallow every last drop of it while Asher moans in the pleasure of the orgasm. "Damn baby, you looked so beautiful taking me into your mouth."

I wipe at the corners of my mouth and when Asher lowers down to kiss me, my bones melt away. I always thought guys had this thing about kissing girls after a blowjob but maybe not all guys have that because Asher's tongue swipes my mouth like he wants to make sure I swallowed every bit of his semen.

"Marry me, Hayley," he whispers on my lips, and I freeze on the spot, suddenly feeling cold.

I look at him in shock and pull away to cover myself with one of the blankets. I don't like where this conversation is going, even less so when I'm naked.

"I will never be a Dawson again, Asher. I can't."

"And you don't have to, baby. I'll take your name. We'll both change it, I don't care," he says and I'm sure I narrow my eyes at him, because he laughs at me.

"Asher Marshall doesn't really work together," I mumble, and he laughs even harder.

"I'm serious, Hayley. I never thought I'd see you again, let alone have this chance. Baby, I love you and have loved you for 4 fucking years and I'm not ashamed to say it. I will never leave you again. Before I was under the impression that if you didn't want anything to do with me anymore, I could let you go, but baby that was a fat fucking lie because after I've had you, I will never be able to let go. Even if you throw me out the door, I'll climb up the window. This, baby, is forever. I swear on my worthless life. Marry me, Hayley."

His speech brings tears to my eyes, and I can't quite believe that this is real.

"Well, technically you're marrying *me*, Mr Marshall," I laugh and place a kiss on his jaw.

"That's true and I couldn't be happier about it. I can't wait to make you my wife, and to treat you like you deserve to be treated, but first, let's burn the Dawson name to the ground." He

We are naked, engaged, and thirsty for revenge.

I think everything I endured was just to lead me to this moment in time, where even after all the pain and suffering, I get my happy ending and Sebastian gets to rot down below.

In the end, I am free, I am alive, and he did not win.

Sebastian Dawson will never get to win again.

"Speaking of burning, I might have an idea," I say with a grin and Asher raises a brow in question. "I know exactly how to end it all and have a new beginning. How to kill this feeling of him being around me still. I'm going to burn down the mansion." I add and Ace remains still for a moment until he returns a grin even bigger than my own.

"Let's fucking do it."

***

It's around 12 am when Asher holds the giant door of the manor open for me and I step inside, while memories flood me like a headrush. I remember the first time I walked into this house and how in an instant I knew it was going to be my prison.

I look up the stairs and can see myself walking down as a bride, soon after Asher took me on Sebastian's desk. I look at the kitchen and see myself taking punches from Sebastian, because dinner wasn't ready, although I wasn't the one that made it.

I look toward the living room, and I see myself

curled up on the sofa, crying for hours on end when he wasn't there to punish me for it.

When Sebastian was around, I was a stone-cold-blooded bitch, as he used to call me because I knew how much he enjoyed inflicting pain and seeing me suffer, but when I was left alone in this beautiful, immense prison, I let my heart pour it all out.

The one thing I am proud of in all these years of abuse is the fact that he never managed to get me pregnant, although he wished to, I was careful to protect myself without his knowing.

"I hope you're enjoying this, you fucking monster," I whisper and spit on the floor like a tomboy.

Asher returns a minute later and looks deep into my eyes. "You ready to do this?"

"Asher... you grew up here," I whisper and shake my head, suddenly feeling nervous.

Maybe taking this away from him is not such a great idea after all.

"This stopped being my home a long time ago, baby. The house of your nightmares will never be my home again, so burn it down!" he says with a grin and hands me a set of matches.

"Can I do it alone, please?"

"Of course, baby, I'll be right outside if you need me. Throw the match right at the curtain, I threw some gasoline on it, so it should light up quicker, and come then out," he instructs me, kisses my forehead, and exits the villa, leaving me with the demons.

You know how they say a soul is trapped in the place they've been killed, now I wish I would've killed him, and he were here to burn with his precious Villa.

I open the matchbox and grab one with trembling fingers. I cross the colored tip over the matchbox and fire sparkles to life before my eyes. I throw the match as instructed and wait for the flames to engulf this terror house. The high window curtains light on fire within seconds and then the fire spreads on the wall through the wallpaper, and the floorboard, and finally, it reaches the sofa and the living room.

I start walking toward the entry door, but I don't leave until smoke starts to hurt my lungs. When I reach the front porch, I leave the door open and stop to listen for the crackling of my freedom.

Four years later, my liberation smells like smoke, sounds like bliss, and tastes like revenge and although they say that revenge is best served cold, man how good it is when it's hot.

"You look like an avenging angel with that background," he whispers on my lips before he gives me a bone-melting kiss. He wraps his arms around me in a protective embrace and his tongue dominates mine with ease. "God, you look so beautiful and hot that I could take you right here," he says in a rush while his hands roam my body, bringing every cell back to life and making it hum with need.

"What's stopping you?" I breathe the words, a way of accepting him and telling him that I want him. I want this to work and I'm willing to give us a real chance.

"Babygirl, if you say that one more time, I'll do things to your tiny body that might hurt you. I won't be able to hold myself back, Hayley, I've missed you too much, baby."

I look deep into his eyes, place both my arms around his neck and repeat in a lustful voice. "What's stopping you?"

Understanding the approval I give him; he takes my hips in his big hands and lifts me off the ground. I quickly wrap my legs around his waist, and he carries me to where the car is, while the flames blaze and tear everything down behind us.

Tonight, I chose to wear jeans so when we reach the car, it takes us a bit of time to get rid of them but once I'm in my underwear, Asher pulls me onto his lap and makes me wrap my legs around him. "Do you remember how you came on my pants back then?"

I nod quickly and I'm sure I blush because he chuckles. "I want you to do it again, baby, but this time I want you to take off your panties," he whispers and then kisses me with hunger. My hips start rolling on his massive cock which I can feel engorged through his pants. The idea of being bare while he's fully clothed makes me go crazy but before I can move aside to undress, he snaps my panties in 2 and lets them fall onto the car floor.

This experience is more intimate than anything else. "Just like that baby," he growls in my ear when I start moaning and the way he thrusts into me makes me lose my mind. Sensing the orgasm inch closer, I attack his lips with ferocity and ride the wave of pleasure as if my life depends on it. We could say it does, because I never thought I'd be able to experience this again.

"God I've missed this. Now it's my turn," he growls when my panting slows down a bit and he throws me on the car seat and settles between my legs with such speed that I get dizzy. He then pulls down his sweatpants and within seconds he fills me up with his thick shaft, making me throw my head back and bite my lip. I wrap my legs around his waist and although I fit on the seat just fine, he has trouble because of his massive build so he keeps one leg on the car floor and one knee on the seat.

I remember the few times we had sex like it was yesterday because I have replayed them in my head over and over again for the past 4 years, but none of them compared to this time where the lust, the need, and the way we missed each other makes us lose our minds. "Damn baby, you fit so well around me. Keep your pussy clenching like that and I'll come before I get to enjoy this."

"You have the rest of our lives to enjoy this, Asher. I'm yours if you want me," I whisper in a strained breath.

"If I want you. Baby, I fucking need you,"

he snarls and pushes even deeper inside of me, hitting that sweet spot that makes my legs shake.

"I'm gonna come, Asher," I breathe as soon as my second climax starts to creep into my bones. With a devilish grin, Asher lifts me up again and before I know it, I'm back on his lap and the way my clit rubs on his skin now is like a drug, so I start rolling my hips into him while he thrusts me deep, creating the perfect movement to send me over the edge.

"Come for me, baby," he pleads, and I unravel in his arms like his whispers were magic. I shudder in his arms and let my climax consume me. "Yes, that's it, Hayley. Take me deep, baby," he adds and comes undone after two deep thrusts.

We stay unmoved for a long time, trying to get control over our breathing. "We should get going before the police find us here. I'm sure firefighters will be here soon if someone reported it," he breaks the silence and I climb off him and grab my jeans.

I jump out of the car giggling and climb onto the passenger seat in the front while Asher takes the wheel and soon after that, drives us into the night, leaving the blaze behind us to swallow all the nightmares, demons, and tears.

HAYLEY

FOUR YEARS AGO

I can't lie and say that I fully understand why Sebastian is so badly against me. I don't get it. Why does he hate me so much?

Tonight, I chose to wear a black, tight dress with a deep and very high opening on my left hip. Strapless and corseted, it gives away very expensive vibes because of the velvety material and it's already turned many heads my way.

I've been here for more than an hour and Asher has disappeared without a trace, promising he'll be back very quickly and asking me not to leave without him, but after the show we'd put on for Sebastian when we arrived, I fear there might be consequences.

"Good evening, Miss Marshall. Delighted to see that you've made it," Sebastian approaches me and I smile politely.

He looks so different from Ash. While Asher's hair color is golden dark blonde and has ocean blue eyes, this man's hair is dark brown with deep chocolate eyes. I would assume that he looks like his mother, because Ash looks like his dad.

"Good evening, Sebastian," I say trying to be

polite, but he kisses my hand way too seductively and I feel like I need to take a step back to make sure he doesn't do anything stupid.

"Let me get you a drink since my brother abandoned you," he adds a second later.

I don't know how to react, so I laugh at his comment. He proceeds to go to the bar to fetch me a drink, while I look around, hoping that Asher will come rescue me soon. I would much rather prefer to spend time with him than with his brother. My wishes don't come true though and Sebastian returns with our drinks and a big smile on his face.

"Cheers," he says and hands me a martini while he's got himself a neat whiskey.

I shouldn't be drinking, but I'm nervous and could use some alcohol to loosen my nerves. Sebastian takes a sip from his drink without taking his eyes off me for a second, and that gives me an unnerving feeling.

We spend some more time in conversation and before I realize it, I become lightheaded and lose my balance for a second. This shouldn't be happening after just one drink and that worries me for a second, but I don't get to do anything about it because a few minutes later I feel the room spinning and darkening around me.

I am vaguely aware of a man's arms around me and although I hope they're Asher's, I have a feeling it's Sebastian and worry takes over my soul.

Did he spike my drink?

Could he stoop so low?

"It's okay. You're going to be okay," he whispers in my ear and leads me away. I try to scream and shout for help, but my mouth seems unable to make a sound. When we reach a door in the hotel where the event is held, he opens it and drags me inside, throwing me on the bed with force.

"What have you done to me?" I manage to whisper before darkness consumes me wholly.

Darkness that tastes like poison.

***

When I open my eyes slowly, I don't know if it's been minutes, hours, or days. My head is pounding, and I find myself wincing because of the bright lights in the room.

I suddenly become aware I'm not alone and when my eyes reach the man standing in front of me with a drink in his hand, fear paralyzes me. I am vaguely aware of him dragging me into this room, but nothing after that.

What shocks and scares me even worse, is the fact that he's in his boxers and his Dress shirt is fully opened.

He smiles at me, and I know something's wrong, so when I look down at my body, I whimper at the sight of my ripped dress. "What did you do to me?" I manage and tears start rolling down my cheeks.

Who is this man? This can't be Sebastian. It has

to be an impersonator or maybe it's just not real.

It can't be real.

Where are you, Asher?

Help me...

"Just because I can, little girl. You think you can swoop in here and fool my brother? A firefighter, really Hayley? You want him to be a goddamn firefighter?" He snarls and throws the glass at my head, barely missing my head.

"What are you talking about?" I whisper with a trembling voice. The lump in my throat gets bigger by the second.

I am vaguely aware that I'm in danger and that I might never make it out of here alive, all because I fell in love.

"I'm talking about all the shit you filled his head with for the past months. The fool is in love with you already and I can't let that happen. We had plans. I had plans that you came in and ruined, so now I'm going to ruin you!"

I'm in such shock that I can barely register everything he's telling me, but I look around trying to analyze the room I'm in because I won't go down without a fight and if all I manage to do is poke his eye out, then I'll be happy.

"He worships the ground you walk on and you..." I release in a broken whisper.

"Shut the fuck up, you stupid whore!" He shouts and I make myself small on the bed.

He is a fucking psychopath and I become more aware of it by the minute.

He starts pacing the room like a maniac and I can't stop shaking.

Why is this happening to me? What did he do to me?

Why do my thighs hurt so bad?

"What did you do to me, Sebastian?" I raise my voice and when he turns his head to look at me, the glimmer in his eyes makes me cower. I shouldn't fight him if I want to get out of this, but I just can't contain my rising anger.

"Nothing, beautiful. I just took what will be mine from now on," he says with a smile and sits on the bed next to me. He reaches my face with his hand, but I slap it away and spit in his face.

"No... you didn't touch me. You wouldn't dare touch me!" I shout and run out of the bed. I reach him after two long strides and slap him hard across the face.

His smile only grows, and he grabs both my wrists to stop me from fighting him. "I did, baby. I did it and it was so good that I am getting hard again thinking about your tight little pussy. I can almost understand why my brother is ready to throw it all away for it," he says with a moan and grabs his groin with his hand, letting out a moan that makes me sick to my stomach and I recoil.

This is sick.

I break free from his grasp and jump off the bed, ready to fight him to the death if needed.

He is sick.

I start shaking my head while tears blur my

vision. "You wouldn't do that to your brother, you psycho!"

Sebastian jumps out of bed with a speed that frightens me and grabs me by my throat, making it really hard to breathe. "I'm doing this *for* him!" He snarls in my face, and I shut my eyes hard. "My brother, my brother. He's not my fucking brother. He's a whore's son. A whore who seduced my father and had him so I will never allow him to have what's supposed to be mine, and that includes you. I need him to go to London so I can have full control of the company and that will never happen if he has you. I have it all on tape, beautiful and if you don't cooperate, I'll first show it to him, and then kill everyone you love, including him, of course. I will torture you in front of him. Fuck you real well and real good in front of him. I'll break his spirit, then yours. I will do things you can't even dream to think about" he adds and throws me back on the bed with ease.

I take a few deep breaths in before I'm able to speak again. "What do you get from doing this to us?"

He seemed delighted by my question and eager to answer. "Two things, baby girl. My brother where I need him to be, as far from here as possible and a 24/7 cocksucker."

"I'll never be your whore puppet." I snarl at him.

"Oh no, baby. I wouldn't want that. You'll be my wife. My perfect, pretty little wife."

His words shock me to the core of my being but

he's messing with me, right? He has to be messing with me because he can't be that deranged.

He can't hope to destroy two lives and have me live perfectly happy with him. I will kill myself before he gets a chance to touch me again.

I clench my teeth hard to keep more tears from falling. "You should be proud of yourself, you fucking monster, but know this, Sebastian. Every time you fuck me, and I have my eyes closed, it's because I'll be thinking of him. I will never love you and I will never look at you the way I look at him and if I ever catch you with your back at me, I'll fucking stab you." I spit in his face while he's getting all red with anger.

The slap that follows hits me so hard that I fall to the floor and stay there, unmoving for a long minute.

My life is over.

FOURTEEN | ASHER

PRESENT DAY

I watch Hayley a she is peacefully sleeping, her head resting on my arm. I still can't believe that she's in my arms again. I still can't believe everything she endured for 3 fucking years. Having to stay away from her for those 3 years has been the hardest thing that I had to do in my entire life, so I am completely shocked that she's sane after all that pain and suffering she had gone through.

I push any thoughts and regret about that at the back of my mind because it'll do no one no good. If I want to make up for everything now, I need to make sure I treat her right, not dwell in the past when the fucker that caused it all is dead.

"You look lost in thought," she says in a sleepy voice and I catch her gaze and smile.

"I was. I'm sorry." I reply and kiss the top of her head.

She sighs and takes my hand into her small palm. "You never told me what some of your tattoos mean."

"They mean a lot of things, and nothing at the same time."

"How about this one?" she asks and places a soft kiss on my fingers.

"They are dates in tribal language," I explain with a cheeky smile, not saying everything just yet.

I like that she wants to know though, however, she didn't notice there's a new tattoo on my ring finger, one which I changed after I'd met her.

She sits up to look me in the eyes. "What dates?" she enquires with a frown.

"Important dates in my life. My mother's passing, my father's. The day we met…"

"The day we met?" she squeaks in shock, bringing out another chuckled laughter from me.

I nod. "The day we met. Right here," I bring my hand up and show her my ring finger where the happiest day of my life rests proudly, and although there were many times when I wanted to go and erase it, something deep down didn't let me.

Her eyes fill instantly with tears and I wipe underneath them with my thumb. "Don't cry, baby. Never again."

She shakes her head. "If these are the tears you'll make me shed from now on, I want them every day, for the rest of my life. Asher, even when you hated me, you still loved me."

"I will love you for every second of my life. Any life. Here and now, and in the after," I confess and grab her face to kiss the lips that haunted my dreams and made me wake up thirsty each night.

She grabs my hair with both hands and her

touch makes me shudder. "Fuuck, baby. Your touch is pure ecstasy and agony, wrapped up in a soft hand. Never take this from me again, you hear me? I will die before I let anyone come between us again," I whisper on her neck and nib at it.

Now it's her turn to shudder and moan, driving me insane and making my boxers suddenly too tight. I jump out of the bed and round it in a second, then I grab her by the waist and lift her up. She wraps her legs around my waist and I head toward my bathroom.

"You know, they say that your peak is in your thirties, and now I know what they mean. I never felt more alive," she whispers on my lips after she's kissed them. Then she kisses my jaw, my cheek, my ear and my head starts spinning.

I enter the shower still holding her tightly against my chest, afraid that if I let go she'll disappear and turn the water on. She jumps off my arms enough to take my boxers off and her T-shirt, so I take advantage and spin her around, to get a view of her beautiful ass.

She's a lot thinner now than she was when I'd met her, when her ass bigger, rounder, but it doesn't mean she's less beautiful. She will always be the most beautiful woman in any room, no matter the shape or weight she has.

I get down on one knee and bite her right cheek right before I grab both of them with my hands and spread them wide, so that I can get access to her sweet holes. Yes, both of them.

"Oh, God, Asher," she whimpers as I spit into her spread asshole and use my index finger to massage it. I push it slowly inside and use my other hand to play on her clit, so that the intrusion on the back end isn't too much for her.

She moans and bucks against my fingers. "You like that baby? You like both of your holes filled?"

"Yes, yes. I need you in there Asher," she says as a plea and my throat goes dry at the invitation. I quickly raise onto my feet, grab my cock with my right hand and guide it at her back entrance, while I still rub her clit with my left one.

I push in just an inch and I feel her muscles lock underneath me. "You okay? Is this okay for you?" I grit out and push another inch in.

"Yes. It's perfect, don't stop," she replies in a breathy moan. I push in bit by bit until I bottom out and then I intensify my thrusts.

"Tell me you want it, baby," I almost snarl as I turn her around and hike up her right leg with my arm so that I get easy access to her burning pussy.

She grabs my shoulder with one arm so she can hold onto something while I find my way toward her wet entrance and start pounding with greed. "I fucking crave it, Asher. I need you more than air." She says and when the climax takes over her thin body she bites down my shoulder to muffle her screams.

"Scream, baby. I want to hear as you as you come undone," I growl and grab her throat to stop her from biting my shoulder.

"Asher... Ace, it's so good. Don't stop. Never stop," she breathes and meets my thrusts, making me spill everything inside of her with a feral snarl and blurred vision.

This is where I want to die.

In her arms. Inside of her.

We remain entangled together against the shower screen while we catch our breaths and my vision returns to normal. "I never thought it can get better, but it seems I was utterly wrong."

Hayley gives me a thumbs up, unable to speak and that makes me laugh wholeheartedly.

God, she's amazing, and she's all mine again.

ASHER

FOUR YEARS AGO

Hayley hasn't been replying to any of my texts or calls. I had to leave her alone at that damn party because my brother decided to be a prick. He said there's an emergency at his fucking club and he couldn't go deal with it himself, so I had to. Now I have a feeling something's wrong with Hayley and curse myself for not taking her with me.

How could I be so fucking stupid! Sebastian is out to break us apart and I left her alone, surrounded by strangers and easily accessible by him.

I just thought that whatever the emergency was, she didn't have to see it and it wouldn't take long to deal with it, but it's been nearly 2 hours and I'm just leaving the club now.

I'm worried sick and I'm sure she does this to spite me for leaving her alone but that's okay because I'll spank the shit out of her later tonight for this.

We pull in front of the hotel where the event is held and I jump out of the car so fast that I might look crazy, but I miss her. I've missed her the entire week and now my asshole brother is trying to keep me away from her. I'll smack his face if he pulls shit like this again.

When I enter the event hall, Milo, Sebastian's assistant greets me, and I get this feeling of unease in the pit of my stomach before he talks. "Sebastian wants to see you, he's waiting for you in room 46."

"I need to find my girl first," I snarl and clench my fist.

"She's there too," he announces and blood rushes to my brain, making me see red.

Why would my girlfriend be in a hotel room with my brother, a man she doesn't like?

I head to the room with my jaw clenched and boiling blood. I knew something was off, damn it! I fucked up for sure.

I can feel it in my bones.

I reach the room in under 30 seconds and when I press the door handle, I notice that my hand is shaking, so I take a deep breath to steady it. I push the door open and when I enter, I find Sebastian and Hayley, hand in hand at the edge of the bed, and my entire world crumbles underneath my feet.

"You two know each other?" It's all I manage to choke out as a lump forms in my throat.

"Ace, I..." she jumps up with tears streaming down her face, but I can't even stand to look at her. Something broke inside me when I saw their linked hands and I can't stand being here anymore. I can't stand seeing them so close to each other but before I leave, I take two large steps toward them and punch my brother in the face with all my strength, making him stagger back a couple of steps and giving him a nosebleed.

I don't know which of them should I be angry with, but it's clear I won't touch her so he's going to have to deal with the punches. "You slept together?"

"Asher, I'm so sorry," she whispers between sobs but that's not confirming or denying anything.

"No, I don't actually want to hear any of it. You two deserve each other," I spit before any of them get to say anything else and I storm out of the room.

I never doubted her, but that's what they do best, isn't it? Manipulate, lie and cheat.

I am such a fucking idiot.

I don't walk downstair, I run because I need something I haven't needed in more than 3 years, alcohol. When I get outside in the crisp air of October, I head straight to the bar down the street, the one that's always welcomed me when I needed it in the past.

I walk inside and I sit at the bar. I flag down the bartender and am surprised to see it's the same guy who used to serve me in the past, but I can't remember his name.

"Asher Dawson, back in my bar, how are you doing, man?" he greets me and hands me a tonic water, which I pass right back.

"Whiskey on the rocks," I say while trying very hard not to tell him to fuck off.

I really can't be friendly right now.

I really can't be civil right now and I understand I shouldn't be around people, so as soon as the guy hands me the whiskey, I down it in one go, place a 20 bill on the bar, and walk out.

The hotel is across the street from the DBSA tower so all I have to do to get home is cross the street but before I do that, I go to my car to ask Eddie a favor.

"Eddie, can you please go buy me a bottle of whiskey and bring it up for me."

"Mr Dawson, are you sure that's a good idea?"

"I'm more than sure, Eddie. You go get me that bottle before I lose my shit. Please and thank you."

Eddie doesn't argue with me anymore and exits the car to go fetch me the alcohol.

I never knew you could get from love to hate so fast, but I just did.

I truly hate her.

FIFTEEN | HAYLEY

PRESENT DAY

"I think it's a good time now to make a press release about everything before we sell everything," I say while I sit back in Asher's comfortable chair.

He nods. "You're absolutely right. I'll ask Mitch to deal with calling the reporters straight away." Asher jumps on his feet and exits the office to go do exactly as he said, so I let my head fall onto the headrest and relax for a bit.

A few minutes later when the door opens and the sound makes me look at the person walking in, my eyebrows shoot up in confusion. "Can I help you, Mickayla?"

I'm left even more shocked when she continues to stroll in like she owns the place and pins me with a mean look. "You may be new pussy for now, but he'll come back to me, just so you know. Don't get too comfortable in that chair."

I look at her wide eyed for a long second before laughter erupts from deep within my soul. She is so damn stupid, it's unbelievable.

I get up from my chair and round the desk to

be able to be eye level with her. "You know, when I first saw you, I knew there couldn't be too much going on in your tiny brain for you to be sleeping with your boss, but I couldn't care less. Now I do. Sweet Mickayla, you're fired and to be quite honest with you, I'm doing you a favor, because we're selling the company for spares anyway." The shocked look on her face thrills me. "Oh, and don't bother going to the press, they're on their way here as we speak. So be a good girl, pack your shit, and make sure we never cross paths again because I won't be as nice."

She huffs an incredulous laugh, spins around and exits the office without another word.

Honestly, I was jealous that Ace was nailing her, and that she got to come on his dick, something that belong to me, but I wouldn't have been so mean if she didn't have the nerve to show up and prove me just how stupid and narrowminded she is.

"They're setting everything up within the hour. We should get some lunch in the meantime," Asher suggests and I nod happily. I am quite happy and should get some food so that I don't throw up on the stage.

***

An hour or so later, when everything is ready for us to take the stand and say what's going to happen next, we exit the restaurant hand in hand and walk toward the stage they quickly put together.

"Ready to do this?" Asher gives me a light squeeze and asks.

I nod. "I've been waiting a long time to do this. I'm so fucking ready!"

He returns a warm smile and as soon as cameras spot us, the lights start flashing. I grip Asher's hand better, and he helps me up the stage first. A second later, after he's taken a spot at my right, he taps the microphone twice and starts speaking. "Good afternoon, everyone. Thank you so much for coming on such short notice. Today I'm going to make some of you very rich, but first, I want you to listen to my fiance very carefully. Yes, some of you know her as Sebastian Dawson's wife, but she was my girlfriend before everything turned very dark. I'm going to let her to tell you the story."

I take a deep breath, step forward and lean down for the microphone to capture my voice very well. "Good afternoon, everyone. I know that Asher's news shocked a lot of you, but after you hear what I have to say, you'll understand. Our story is long, heart breaking and horrible, so I'll try to be as quick as possible. It's important you write down everything, because it's just as important that you understand who the bad guy is, and that is Sebastian Dawson. Four years ago, I met Asher and we quickly fell for one another, that ruining some of Sebastian's plans for his brother. At first, he tried to break us up through lies and games, but when that didn't work, he went a different way. Sebastian Dawson drugged and raped me on

July 26th, a few weeks before we got married. We were at a company event where Asher invited me so that we can show Sebastian that his plans won't work. Before you ask why I didn't speak up at the time, the answer it's simple. I was young, alone and scared. Sebastian swore he would show videos of us together to Asher and eventually kill him if I didn't play along to his horrible plan, so I did. I squashed everything deep inside and played along so that my soul mate, a man that I'm sure I loved in every life before, would live even if it meant he'd hate me."

I take a break to breathe and wipe my teary eyes, before continuing. "I won't go ahead and speak of every terrible thing that Sebastian Dawson did to me after we got married, at least not today, but I will tell you that freedom is a blessing not every woman in an abusive relationship gets. So, I'm going to do what I can to help, starting with selling the Dawson Company for spares. That being said, let it be known that DBS is now open for auction, but we will only consider bids that involve tearing the company down and turning it into something else. All proceeds will go to abused women's shelters. This is all for now and please if you have questions, make them short. Thank you."

A few hands shoot up, so I choose a woman to speak. "Miss Hayley, is it true that you were supposed to be in the car with Sebastian Dawson on the night of his accident?"

"That's true. We were supposed to attend that

evening like the happy couple he liked to parade around, but he beat me up so badly that night that no make-up could cover my swollen and bruised face, so I stayed home instead." I divulge some of the truth that only 3 people know now.

Asher held his hand at the small of my back as reassurance the entire time I spoke. I choose a man for the next question.

"Mister Dawson, DBSA is your father's legacy. How did she convinced you to agree to sell it for spares?" He asks and points his recorder at us.

Asher takes a step forward and speaks. "She didn't have to convince me at all. I will gladly get rid of the Dawson name after everything she had to endure for me. As a matter of fact, I am also changing my name, because as soon as get married, I will take her name. I will make sure that the Dawson name is reduced to nothing in this city. That would be all for now. Thank you."

Everyone gasps and starts whispering when they hear what Asher says but I can barely contain my smile as he grabs my hand again and we get off the small stage.

May hell torture your soul forever, Sebastian Dawson.

HAYLEY

FOUR YEARS AGO

I'm still curled up on the bed when Sebastian enters the room again, but I refuse to lift my eyes and look at him. He strolls into the room, and I feel his eyes on me for a long time before he speaks. "Did you memorize the story?"

I ignore him, all lost in my head.

The look of pure agony is Asher's eyes when he saw me with his brother, still haunts my vision. It probably will for the rest of my days.

"Answer me!" He shouts next and takes a few steps toward me, so I lift my eyes to meet his. I'm not trying to defy him and make it worse, but I'm just exhausted.

I'm so exhausted.

A second later, I nod with a clenched jaw, and I bite the inside of my cheek to keep my damn mouth from saying something it shouldn't.

"Good, let's go then."

"Sebastian this madness has to stop. I won't see him, I promise, but I'm not marrying you. I'm going home," I say with a sigh and jump off the bed.

Before I can register what's happening to me,

Sebastian backhands me so hard that stars explode and my vision blurs. I can tell my lip is also split by the coppery taste I get on my tongue. He then proceeds to grab my arm and squeeze it tightly before throwing me on the bed like a doll. I am so shocked by his outburst that the only thing I manage to do is take a hand to my burning cheek and rub it slowly. "You are going to be my wife, no questions asked. You go home or even pick up a call from that little friend of yours, and I'll make sure they never see sunlight again. Got it, beautiful?"

"Sebastian, you're forcing me to marry you, after you've just forced yourself onto me. How do you expect this to work?" I reply with a heavy swallow.

"You should've never even looked his way. This is all your fault," he blames me and motions for me to get up. "Now I want you to put this on even if we go through the back door," he adds while he hands me his long coat to cover my ripped dress.

Am I really going to stay quiet? Am I really going to go home with him tonight, after what he's done to me? Do I even have another option, when Jennifer and Asher are involved?

Asher... what he must think of me. How much he must hate me for something I didn't do.

***

It's been a little over a week since I was forced to move into Sebastian's mansion and here I am, in a damn wedding dress, close to saying yes to the bastard who hits me 3 times a day like clockwork and takes me raw every night.

How could I end up in this mess? How can I ever get out of it without losing the only two people I love and have in my life?

Sebastian forced me to cut contact with my best friend and any other friends I had while he also forbade me to go to College. He took control of my life with an iron grip and is controlling every second of it, leaving me unable to even think of a way out before it's too late.

I try my best to not show any emotion while people are around me. They can't see me breaking down. He can't see me break down because he thrives on it. It's when he likes to take me the most, when I beg him to stop, so now I just don't anymore.

In just one week, I lost all my fight.

I look at myself in the mirror and a sad smile stretches on my lips. I used to dream about being a bride, but I never thought that my dream would turn into a nightmare. I never thought that the beginning of a love story could take such a horrific turn and what's worse, is that I have no one in my corner. He will never allow anyone in my corner from now on. Isn't that what abusers do?

My wedding dress is a short satin bodycon dress, with long sleeves that Sebastian picked up for me to wear. Even if I would've wanted to pick the dress myself, he never would've allowed it because there had to be something that covered anything that the makeup wouldn't.

Lost in thought, I never noticed Asher watching me closely and when our eyes meet in the mirror, a sob escapes from my lips. "You shouldn't be here... he promised."

"What else did he promise you?" He retorts with a stone set jaw and hardened gaze,

I bite my tongue. "Everything I ever wanted," I utter, and a tear rolls down my cheek, confusing him. I avert my gaze and wipe the tear away.

"Do you love him? How do you even know him?" he fires questions at me that I don't have answers for. Not what he's seeking anyway.

I can't utter those sadistic words, so I just nod, completely ignoring the second question. I know the script, but would he even believe that stupid story?

I can't risk it.

He steps closer and I have to close my eyes in order to control my beating heart. Don't do this... don't torture me, Ace. I don't deserve this.

I don't deserve any of it and yet, here we fucking are.

"You want me to suddenly believe you love him? You're going to have to learn to control your reactions. You love *me*, admit it, and end this charade!" He growls and spins me around so fast that I get lightheaded and have to grab a hold of his arms to steady myself.

"We are over, Asher," it's all I say, and take two steps backward to put some distance between us. He's not helping my situation by getting so close in my face. I'm a word away from a meltdown and he can't see it.

I can't risk it.

When Asher's hand reaches down my thigh and brings my dress up in a slow painful movement, my breath hitches in my throat.

"If you love him so much, why do you shiver under my touch?" he whispers in my ear, and I shut my eyes tightly to block him out.

I can't listen to his torture but when his hand reaches the belting of my underwear, I think I forget how to breathe altogether and even though I should stop him before this turns into a whole different nightmare, I don't.

I can't.

I'm frozen with desire and need.

Knowing that this is the last time he'll ever touch me, I block all reason out and bathe myself in the sensations he provokes with a single stroke of his finger.

When he reaches my throat with his left hand and my burning clit with his right one, I shudder a breath and lean onto him for support.

"This is not the reaction a woman about to get married should have, Hayley," he barks and inserts a finger inside me, making me whimper. "Are you a whore, Hayley? Is that why you're doing this?" he adds and his left hand travels down to cup my breast, so I quickly nod, not wanting him to stop. He then thrusts into me to show me what I do to him like this is all my fault.

If I would be able to have him like this every time Sebastian abuses me, then I might be able to live with it. If bliss came after horror, I would take it.

"I need you to say it, baby," he snarls and pinches my nipple through my dress and lace bra.

"Yes, I'm a whore," I release in a breath and buck my hips to meet his working fingers. Asher growls and he suddenly leaves my aching core to push me onto the small desk in the room, still keeping me with my back to him. I gasp in surprize and brace myself before I hit the hard surface, but he doesn't give me any time to think this through before he pushes my dress on my hips and works to release the beast in his pants.

"Then you're going to take it like a whore," he spits and enters me in a hard rushed thrust but I'm so wet that it just makes me moan loudly. "And then you're going to remember that on your wedding day, I fucked you first, then your husband," he adds as he picks up the pace, slamming into me with rage and although his words hurt me, he pleases me where it matters the most right now. I moan and when the sweet orgasm rolls through me, I start crying in both pleasure and pain. After a few deep thrusts, Asher follows me with his release groaning and cursing my name under his breath.

Then he exits me, leaving me bare on the desk, unable to move.

When I become aware of what I just did, I sit up straight, arrange my dress, and wipe the tears away from my cheeks.

"You are just another whore, isn't it?" he spits with rage while tucking himself back in his pants and the hurt and disappointment in his eyes are utterly breaking my soul, not only my heart.

"Don't do this, Asher, please. We haven't known each other for long but I think it was long enough to care for each other, enough to not be this cruel to one another," I whisper, and tears roll down my cheeks, making it impossible to stop them.

His words are breaking me all over again.

"You wanna talk about cruelty, talk about marrying my brother. You took my fucking heart and stomped on it with a smile on your face, Hayley. I can barely even look at you anymore."

His words hurt me to the depths of my bruised soul and I'm sure they'll echo in my head for the rest of my miserable life, but it's best if he hates me. He'll suffer less.

"Have a nice life, Hayley." He throws without any sight of emotion in his eyes.

And just like that he turns around and walks away, leaving me for the monster to devour me.

Leaving me alone to suffer because I was foolish enough to think I could be part of a love story when it's clear I'm meant to be part of a nightmare instead.

SIXTEEN | ASHER

PRESENT DAY

"I just can't believe how fast everything was." Hayley whispers from my right, her head resting on my shoulder.

I nod. I know she means the auction of the company. She sold her part to two buyers, and I sold mine to another two. We signed the papers a few hours ago, and we're now lounging on my penthouse terrace, enjoying the sunset before the buyers come to sign the lease tomorrow. "It's done, baby. A few more days and we'll get as far away from here as possible."

"You know Jen wants to move to New York? I'm just happy I never have to come back here."

I try as much as possible to not live in the past and let everything haunt me, because she won't. Hayley wants to forget and move on, and so do I. At first the rage and guilt overtook my emotions every few minutes, but now every time it surges, I push it down.

I want to build a future with the woman I have loved for 4 years, not live and what I could've done differently.

Now that the sale is finally done, she donated

most of the money to the charities she promised to help. She also wanted to open a foundation for the same purpose, but then that would mean she has to retell and relive everything, which isn't something we want.

Forgetting isn't possible, but neither is healing if you reopen the wound, so she chose to be done with it, because in the end, every time you say Sebastian's name, he's still winning, and we need him to be forgotten.

I'd erase history if I'd be able to, in order to make sure he is a nobody.

"Do you have a place in mind?" I ask about where we should move.

"I always wanted a quiet home on the beach. You know? Like the one in 'The last song'?" I wish I did, but I don't know the movie she mentions.

I nod. "Let's watch it then, and I'll build it for you."

She jumps off the outdoors sofa to look at me. "You'll *build* it?" She asks with a frown, making me chuckle.

"Yes, Hayley. I'll build it. I'm not just some corporate goon, you know? I have other skills and talents." I retort and gesture for her to sit back down.

She grins widely and bites her bottom lip. "I can confirm some of your *skills* and *talents*."

I laugh wholeheartedly and grab her wrist to bring her into my arms. "Malibu, then?"

"Sounds perfect, almost too perfect. Are you

even real?" She whispers so close to my lips that I get lost in her scent.

"Kiss me and find out," I retort and hold her hungry gaze. I'm sure it reflects mine perfectly because I can't get enough of her.

I never will.

She smashes her lips onto mine and dominates me with tongue swirls and an iron grip on my jaw and hair. And I let her.

God, I'd let this woman ruin me over and over again if it means our reunion will be so sweet and passionate.

ASHER

FOUR YEARS AGO

I never meant to get angry and show up on their wedding day, because I knew that wouldn't help me. I never meant to throw those words at her or take her raw while she wore a wedding dress for him, but I couldn't stop myself. Seeing her in that white satin dress, all nice and pretty for him, made me lose my mind. It made me lose control like never before.

I wanted to hurt her like she hurt me, and now I know exactly how to do it.

I finish drinking the rest of my whiskey, set the glass on the table, and head toward the elevator. I know it's quite late and because it's been 3 days since the wedding, I hope they haven't left on their honeymoon, because I'm really thirsty for revenge and I want to ruin it for them.

I want to make her pay and see her crumble when I tell my brother what we did before she said yes to him.

When I reach Eddie downstairs, I climb onto the back seat and bark at him. "Take me to the manor please, I have a gift for the newlyweds."

About 30 minutes later, we park in front of the

house, and I jump out of the car so fast, you'd think my life depends on it, but man, I'm angry. When I reach the door, I decide to knock loudly instead of ringing the bell and the fact that it's 10 P.M., makes me grin wickedly.

My brother always had a live-in maid so when Carla opens the door with a frown, I say good evening and enter the house. "I need to speak to my brother," I say to the maid but when Sebastian descends the stairs, she disappears from sight. He is not in his pyjamas yet, which means he was probably working. After all, he is obsessed with this damn company.

"Asher, what are you doing here at this hour?" he asks with a bored tone but I'm completely speechless when Hayley appears on top of the stairs, in her nightgown. All thoughts flee my mind the second my eyes land on her and I completely forget why I came here for a moment.

"There's something I have to talk to you about," I say through clenched teeth. "But that involves a lot of whiskey, can I get some?" I add when my brother lifts his gaze up the stairs and frowns when he sees his wife. God, the word is so bitter on my tongue that I almost want to throw up.

"Let's go in my office then," he gestures toward the room I know all too well, after all, I grew up in this house.

"Oh, how poetic," I say and throw another quick glance at Hayley, whose eyes are now wide open, like she's terrified of what I'm going to do. Well, she should be. She's a fucking cheater.

When we reach the office, Sebastian fills two glasses and hands me one before he takes a seat at the large brown oak desk. I, however, decide not to sit.

"What's so pressing that it couldn't wait until tomorrow, brother?" he asks with a sigh, but I remain quiet for a long time.

The horror in her eyes, probably thinking that I'd ruin the marriage before they even got a chance. I wanted to hurt her so badly, but am I willing to hurt my brother in the process too? "I, umm, I want to move to London. Everything is just a bit much, brother. I'm glad that you're happy, but I can't be around for that happiness, and I'm sure you understand why." I choose to use a half-lie and keep the truth to myself.

It's best for all of us if I'm not around.

"Of course, you have feelings for her. I hope you know that this is not how I wanted things to turn out for us," he replies with understanding in his eyes. "You know I always wanted you to run the London division, so I'm glad you came to your senses," he jokes and raises his glass for me.

I do the same and take a gulp of my drink, while my gaze doesn't leave Sebastian's. There's something in his eyes I can't quite read and that

"I'll book a flight first thing tomorrow."

"That's great news," he cheers me on with a smile.

"Why are you so eager to see me gone?" I say

with a laugh, but it's not entirely a joke. Something is off about my brother, and I can't understand what that is.

But after all, when was it easy to understand my brother?

SEVENTEEN | HAYLEY

PRESENT DAY

I look at Asher in his beautiful black tux and I still can't believe we've made it this far. He holds my hands in his and I feel just how sweaty they are underneath my touch. I feel just how nervous and happy he is, mirroring my exact feelings.

The first and the last man I'll ever love.

My husband.

We're holding a ceremony on an empty hill, just the two of us underneath the spring sun and I feel like my heart could burst at any minute because of the happiness. We married a few days ago, but today is about having this moment for us, and no one else.

I am so happy it hurts.

"I'm still afraid that at some point I will wake up and all of it would've been just a dream." I whisper and try to swallow the fear.

I'm trying really hard not to let it ruin this beautiful day, but my heart refuses to cooperate with me.

Asher takes my left hand, where there is a beautiful ring resting on my finger and places it on his fast beating heart. "Do you feel that?"

I nod and shiver.

"I am here and I am real and I'm not going anywhere, ever again. I'd rather die before I let anyone break us apart again," he tries to assure me. I lift the left corner of my mouth in the attempt of a smile and he caresses my cheek with his thumb. "If everything that we went through taught me anything is that love isn't something you deserve, but something you earn and you learn to protect no matter the price. I will love and cherish you until my last breath, that's my vow."

When he finishes talking, my eyes are already red and stingy from the tears gathered. "How am I supposed to top that?" I laugh and wipe away at the corner of my eyes.

"I don't need words, you've more than proven your love for me."

I smile. "I still don't feel like it's enough because none of it was any of our fault. We were both just players in a horrible game led by your brother. None of us deserved what happened to us, but I wouldn't change it for the world. We are who we are today in spite of everything and because of everything and I don't want anything to be any different. I love you so damn much that the happiness that I feel today physically hurts."

I sniffle and Asher brings me into his arms with ease. He holds me close to his heart for several minutes before we break apart. I open my mouth to speak again when a set of clapping hands make me stop and turn to see who the owner is. When my eyes land on the man approaching us with a wide grin on his face, my blood turns cold in my veins and my vision blurs.

I quickly reach a hand back toward Asher to make sure that this is real and I'm not having a bad dream and when I tear my gaze away from the devil just to confirm that my husband is seeing what I'm seeing, the rage and fury in his eyes brings all my nightmares to life.

"No..." I manage a cracked whisper. "How is this possible? You're dead. You're supposed to be dead!"

"You motherfucker!" Asher reacts first and before I get to stop him, he takes of and punches Sebastian's smug face with full force. "My wish came true. I get to kill you after all."

I watch the scene frozen on the spot as Asher is being throws off his brother and punched in the gut. A second later they both stand on their feet and continue to throw punches.

"I should've known that you were a psychopath since you killed mom's cat," Asher shouts and punches Sebastian in the face.

"You have no idea what I'm capable of." What his brother does next, however, sets me into motion. When Sebastian brings out a gun from his back and points it at my husband, my entire body feels light and I don't even realize when I've moved and am now standing in front of Asher.

I'm not losing him, not again.

Never again.

"If you think you're going to win again, you are

sadly mistaken." I grit through clenched teeth just as the tip of the gun touches my chest.

"Hayley, no!" Asher grabs my elbow and steps in front of me.

Sebastian laughs at the scene, making me feel nauseated. "Oh, how cute. I loved watching you love birds reunite. You have no idea how excited I was for this moment to finally happen."

"Why? What did I ever did to you?" Asher asks, but doesn't move anymore, aware that if he lets go of me, I'm going to jump in front of a bullet if I have to.

Sebastian's answer is a sick grin. "Your whore of a mother was the start of everything. She took my mother away from me!"

"Sebastian, your mother killed herself," is my husbands reply toward his brother and I just realize that I never knew the whole story myself.

"Because of Moira!" Sebastian shouts and I swallow the fear that's taken over my heart. Then I wipe away the tears that fall uncontrollably on my cheeks and realize that I've also started shivering.

Asher's eyes widen. "Sebastian, they were separated when mom met dad. Your mom has problems, just like you. Your making shit up."

"This is all your fault. You should've gone to London as planned and none of this would've happened. Hayley would have never suffered if you just did what you were supposed to do, *brother*. Now it's too late. I'm done watching you two being happy. She's never going to be yours!" he spits at

Asher and before any of us reacts, Sebastian pulled the trigger and the deadly shot resounds in the empty, now darkening valley.

My eyes widen, my heart races and my mouth opens to scream, but no sound comes out.

Asher drops to the ground, hand clenched over his heart and my own stops beating when blood starts pooling from his mouth. "No, no, no. What have you done? What have you done?" I shout at Sebastian while I drop onto my knees to hold Asher.

This can't be happening. This isn't happening.

"Ace? Don't leave me, please. This isn't how it's supposed to end." I sniffle and caress his cheek.

He opens his mouth and struggles to speak. "Fight him. This time you fight him, you hear me?"

"I will. I will, I'll get you help. You'll be okay, baby," I stutter as Asher's face drains its color. I lean down to kiss his lips but before I reach them Sebastian grabs my elbow and lurches me on my feet.

Sebastian throws one last look at his brother and spits next to him. "You really thought I'd go down so easy, brother?"

When I drop my eyes, I see the hand holding the gun relaxed at his side, and I grab it before I let myself think about it or about the consequences. I quickly take a few paces back and point it at him.

"Maybe you didn't go down the last time, but you are today. Call 911!" I shout and shake the gun in my hands.

I'd never used one before, but I'd seen enough movies to be able to arm it and shoot at his head.

"I won't do shit, just like you won't shoot me, because if you miss, I'll torture you for the rest of your life. That's a promise." He replies with a smirk and my heart squeezes in my chest.

I won't miss.

I want to look at Asher, but I'm not stupid enough to risk taking my eyes off of Sebastian. "You'd love that, wouldn't you? But I won't give the chance, because while my soul mate is fading, I know one thing for sure. I'll never let you win again. I'll never let you have me if there's no one that I need to fight for."

"Don't be stupid, Hayley. You can't kill me. You can't live with it!" he drawls and takes a step closer, so I shoot his right leg, making him crouch down and yelp in pain.

I throw an eye at Asher and see him struggling to breathe. "There's only one way this can end, Sebastian and you're not alive at the end of the story. There's only one way we can be free and happy without having to worry that you'll find ways to trick us again.

"This is your last chance to give me the gun before I lay you on the ground next to my brother. Give it back, Hayley. Give it back and maybe I'll let you save my brother," he says with an edgy tone but all I do is smile.

I'm not afraid.

I will not be afraid.

This is the only way.

I grin widely and pull the trigger again, this time getting him in the arm. "I will not let you win this time. You're dying, for good this time, Sebastian. You will die and I'll be the last face you saw before hell swallows you because that's the only way we can both be free of you and even though that won't happen in this life, I trust and believe we will find each other again."

I pull the trigger again, and this time I aim for his head. I miss, so I aim again, the bullet finding it's way through Sebastian's skull. He collapses with a loud thud and I remain frozen on the spot for a short minute as I draw my breath.

I just killed someone, and I'm about to take one more life.

Mine.

I take a few steps closer to Sebastian's limp body and shoot him again, to make sure that he's gone, then I turn around and run toward Asher. I lower myself near his pale face to listen for breathing, but nothing comes out through his parted blue lips. "I'm going to find you, baby. I promise. I'll always find you, my Ace." I whisper, place a soft kiss onto his cold lips and pull the trigger once more, this time aimed toward my head.

ACKNOWLEDGEMENTS

I can't believe it's finally here. After many sleepless nights, and tired hours after work trying to jot this down, my first book is finally here, so here we are.

Firstly, I want to thank you from the bottom of my heart for giving this book a shot, because if you're reading this bit, then you probably read the chapters too, and for that, I'm grateful to you. I hope you enjoyed Hayley's and Asher's story as much as I did.

Secondly, I want to thank my number one supporter, she knows who she is, the first person to read it, and give me an honest opinion that helped this beauty shape into what it's turned out to be.

ALSO BY ANNA-KAT TAYLOR

Perfect Scars – A Dark Romance Novel

https://www.goodreads.com/book/show/209187108-perfect-scars

&
You Owe Me | Heartbreak High
1 – A Romance Novel

https://www.goodreads.com/book/show/214381983-you-owe-me

Both on Amazon Kindle Unlimited and TIKTOK Shop as a Signed Paperback.

Printed in Great Britain
by Amazon

EPILOGUE

I open my eyes and I'm suddenly greeted by a warm sun and the smell of lavender. It takes me a short moment to get used to the sudden light, but when my eyes get accustomed, I raise on my butt and look around me only to find that I'm surrounded by acres of lavender.

I frown, unable to understand where I am or to remember how I got here, so I stand on my feet and search my surroundings again. I find a path that leads to a house far away, so I start walking slowly towards it.

When I make it close enough to see the layout and if there is anyone inside, a familiar face greets me from the porch with a wide smile.

The man waving at me is dressed in a white pair of shorts and dress shirt, and when our eyes collide, the memories of the events from the last few months flood me and my heart clenches painfully.

"Asher," I breathe and break off into a sprint towards my soul mate. "I told you I'd find you."

"You did," he chuckles and opens his arms for me.

I grab him without hesitation and press my lips

onto his with hunger and passion. Asher returns the kiss in the same manner as I melt into his embrace and take everything from him. Our tongues battle with need like we'd been apart for years, not a few minutes.

When I step away to draw a breath, Asher grins. "You shouldn't have…" I stop him before he finishes the sentence. "Don't say it. I didn't do it for you, I did it for me. Okay? It was the only way, and I wouldn't change a thing. We're together, aren't we? We did it, Asher. We're finally free."

"I love you, Hayley. I will love you for a thousand lives if God grants them to me," he whispers close to my lips. I grin in response and rest my head on his chest.

He knows I love him.

God knows I love him, because we wouldn't be here if he didn't.

We got our heaven and nothing else matters.

The end.